RENAISSANCE

The Nora White Story – Book One

YECHEILYAH YSRAYL

Literary Korner Publishing

For information contact :

Yecheilyah Ysrayl

PO BOX 4662, Shreveport, LA 71134

http://www.yecheilyahysrayl.com

Cover Design : Brick-a-Brack Photography

Cover by Najla Qamber

Edited by Cynthia Brooks

First Edition : July, 2017

10 9 8 7 6 5 4 3 2 1

FROM THE AUTHOR OF

THE STELLA TRILOGY

"When I finished reading *Renaissance: The Nora White Story* I actually shouted. I loved, loved this book, from the beginning to the end. The characters were alive inside my mind. The setting as well. I could smell the hot soup the girls had or the rain on the hot earth. The dialogue is superb; I could and still can hear the soft southern accent in my mind."

- Adele Marie Park

"The author's writing is beautiful. She captivates the dialect of the southern speak wonderfully and I found the description of each and every action and location to just roll off my tongue as I read."

- Rachel Poli

"The author really did her research, touching on the feud between Zora and Langston over a play written by both, but only Zora was given credit. The way she wove Nora into the middle of the feud was genius. It was reminiscent of Forrest Gump a bit. (That, in my world is a HUGE compliment – I love Forrest Gump)"

– Lisa W. Tetting

"First of all, let me say that I'm loving your book so far. The voice (yours/Nora's), imagery, dialogue, and overall literary style remind me of Toni Morrison's…. Damn, girl! You're giving me goals!"

– Nadine Tomlinson

CHAPTER ONE

December, 1923

WHATEVER THE REASON, THERE WASN'T ANYTHING SPECIAL about the first time she saw her. It wasn't just because their names matched or their passions either. It could have had something to do with their roots, how they were both sown in the South and knew the mind of a mule; could have been their stubborn ways and an iron-like fist in their throats; could have been the instability of their youth. Or how they sojourned the world unapologetically, wrapped themselves in rainbows and soared like butterflies trapped in cages. Could have been the giggles in their stomachs and how they burst forth without warning and full of pride.

"I got a woman, she shake like jelly all over. I got a woman, she shake like jelly all over." The passengers perked up in awe at the sound of the couple boarding the train. White women scowled, and Nora put the book face down in her lap and sighed. She was not going to get any reading done this trip. First of all, the woman's voice was irritating. It burst forward like clanging cymbals and sounding brass instruments from deep down in her stomach. It wasn't her voice exactly. The woman, whoever she was, could sing- technically- but she was loud. In fact, she sounded just like Nora's mother, and perhaps that is why it bothered her so. And then there was that feather on her hat that looked like it wanted to float away, and there was absolutely no color in the woman's clothes.

Nora could never get why Northerners were so plain; blacks and grays and blues. And even the blues weren't the color of the sky, but dark and lonesome-like. It was depressing. She wanted to go through the city with cans of white paint and pierce the darkness.

"Girl you just country! We don't like all those loud colors."

Nora chuckled at her friend's voice in her head. She sure did miss Mom and Dad, and even though Walter and Eddy got on her nerves, she missed them too. She didn't know what she would have done without Lisa's help those first few months. Brushing away the thoughts, Nora looked the woman over again. There was something familiar about her that she couldn't put her finger on. *At least her coat is decent. Who is that white man though?,* she thought as the train ripped through the Grizzly Bear's mouth.

Grizzly Bear is what Nora nicknamed the cold. Northern weather was something she could never get used to. It sank its teeth into your skin and gnawed the bone, although the inquisitiveness of the people did make up for it. The city never slept, and it seemed the people didn't either. Speaking of people, back to the colored woman over there singing to the tall white man in the white people's section like she was too good to sit in the back like the rest of them. Nora knew that things were different in the

North, but she was still not used to the sugar coating of the colored line. To Nora, this was worse than full blown racism. The white people here made it clear Negroes were not welcomed except they needed them too much to say anything out loud. Who else was gonna clean their toilets and teach their daughters about their first periods while their mothers went shopping for things?

Nora's thoughts may have something to do with the fact she was Charlotte Crosby's maid, the most racist woman in all creation. She hated to think her parents were right and hoped she didn't have to return to Jackson to hear about it. Mother had already written a dozen letters about how much she missed her and how she wished she'd come home. Nora smirked, *Mama so dramatic.* She had to understand eventually that she was not her little girl anymore.

"So, is that one of those respectable lady songs?" The white man spoke.

Good, thought Nora, *Maybe he'll quiet his friend.*

"Naw, see this here a juke song. Ain't for the respectable ladies, this for the juke."

Nora rolled her eyes and smirked. The lady was kind of funny; another one of her mother's traits. Could that be why she was so familiar? Nora knew she'd seen her somewhere, but where?

"Speaking of respect, you tell that Langston of yours that if he has any more to say about that situation, I don't believe my address is any different. Writing all them letters and such, how comes I ain't got one?"

Nora imagined that if she was a dog with long ears they would now be standing erect and her tail would be wagging. *Did she just say Langston? No, couldn't be. Could it?* Nora thought about how many Langstons were in New York. *I'm sure there are hundreds*, she reasoned.

"AND you can also tell Mr. Hughes that I have no control over the actions and feelings of his patron, and I certainly didn't give her instructions on what we should be paid."

Nora's heart stopped beating and she thought she'd die if she held her breath in any longer.

A colored male passenger looked at Nora, "Ma'am, you alright?

Nora's eyes shifted and her knees bounced up and down to the rhythm of the train, her fingers drumming their excitement on her thighs, "Yes, yes sir I'm fine."

The train stopped and released the loud woman and her white friend. But Nora was not at all content and tried to shake her head loose of the excitement still rolling around in her heart and bouncing up and down in her chest. She looked around at the passengers, all content in their own thoughts as their bodies jerked, bobbing back and forth to the motion of the train. Everyone was back to their frowns, their pushing, elbowing, and squeezing into seats that provided no comfort on the crowded train. *Was that her? Couldn't be*, thought Nora.

CHAPTER TWO

JACOBSVILLE, NEW YORK WAS A 45-MINUTE RIDE FROM HARLEM and had that small-town country feel to it that made Nora comfortable. At the same time, it was a busy city because of its proximity to Harlem. The streets were never empty, and at night the juke joints, quarter parties, and Jazz clubs lit up like the stars congregating in the sky. The morning was a time for the usual hustle and bustle, but at night Negroes parked their cars in the middle of the street and danced until they had enough quarters to pay this month's rent. It was "Little Harlem", and Whites and Negroes alike twisted and spun and split their faces in half with laughter that seemed to forget that sunrise was on its way back to its usual position. The sun was an overseer whipping everyone back into shape. It struck the concrete with light and exposed all the paper bags loitered on the sidewalks and returned everyone to their small corners of the world until it was time to turn its back

—

once again.

"You're late. Again."

Charlotte Crosby rolled her eyes and blew cigarette smoke in the wind, creating little circles with her finger before walking away, leaving the front door to hang open. Nora walked in.

"I'm really sorry ma'am, the..."

"Train. Yes, I know," Crosby interrupted and glided over to her throne of a chair, a gold finish porter with black vinyl, balloon bonnet canopy dome two feet off the floor. She wasn't a beautiful woman, but her money more than made up for it. Charlotte dripped in the kind of fabric that reminded Nora of Southern Whites with enough slave money for several lifetimes. She remembered their first encounter and couldn't miss the way the cotton clung to the woman's body like the dripping moss of trees, clingy and heavy with moisture. Nora laughed to herself about the way the garments weighed down her mistress, bowing to her tree branch arms. It didn't help that she piled make-up on her face either. A mask it was, addicting the soft milky texture of her skin to a chalky pale with sagging cheeks and dark lines around the eyes when she woke up without a hit. Bright red lipstick and green eyeliner didn't mesh well and took away from her ocean blue eyes. It also didn't help that the woman smoked cigarettes like they were going to run out tomorrow. She did have gorgeous reddish hair, though, that hung snug at the shoulders that she didn't seem to like as much as Nora did. Like now, she's got it hidden underneath a platinum night scarf made of silk. The woman may not have had the looks but she had the taste. The matching robe and lace night gown underneath it was stunning. Nora quickly observed that Miss

Charlotte was still in her pajamas at one o'clock in the afternoon.

"So, I hear you're a writer. Do I hear correct or is this a rumor?"

Nora busied herself with the apron she was tying around her waist. She'd become accustomed to multitasking. Rent was due on the first, so she was more concerned with the coffee that needed brewing, the floor that she was sure needed scrubbing, and the dishes she was certain piled themselves to the heavens in that gorgeous sink after another one of Charlotte's late nights. Poor sink. Nothing that beautiful deserved to be neglected in such a way.

"I write, yes."

"Good. Then you should try coming up with better excuses."

Nora walked off. "Give me a break."

"What was that?"

"Coffee ma'am?" Nora spoke with laughter in her voice before the doorbell rang.

"I'm not trying to hear it today, Miss Charlotte," Lisa closed the door behind her. Nora walked over, and the two women hugged.

"Hey girl."

"You just in time too."

Charlotte sucked on the cigarette again before tapping it against the round metal ashtray with the scalloped edge, molded designs and gold foil, and rolled her eyes as Lisa unraveled her scarf and removed her coat before tying on her apron.

"You have your coffee yet, Miss Charlotte?"

"No," said Charlotte, staring at Nora, "your friend here was late again."

Lisa walked up to Charlotte's throne, emptied the ashtray into the small trash can, replaced the half empty pack of cigarettes with a fresh one, and linked arms with Nora as they both disappeared into the kitchen. Nora picked up the broom and began sweeping as Lisa prepared the coffee.

"How do you deal with Charlotte?"

"You mean how Charlotte deals with me."

Nora laughed, "See, that's what I mean. How do you keep your cool like that? That woman be having me about to throw something. And if she calls me girl one more time."

"I thought you'd be used to it, Southerner," said Lisa, winking.

"That's just it. Negroes and Whites don't mix down there. We stay in our place, and as long as they stay in theirs, we good."

"Well up here we work together and that's what you gotta understand. They may not admit it, but they need us just as much as we need them. They just ain't figured it out yet. As much as Miss Charlotte whines and complains, she ain't never gonna wash her own draws or sweep her own floors. Besides, she need somebody to give her money to, may as well be us."

Lisa pulled a large pot from one of the wood cabinets and filled it with water. Nora put the broom to the side, and together they carried the large water-filled pot over to the white porcelain stove. Nora went to scrubbing the floor with the crisp white shine as Lisa turned the silver knobs on the stove, and watched as the fire awakened to attack the bottom of the pot.

"Alright, let me hear it girl."

"Can't," said Nora, standing. It was the table's turn to be scrubbed. Not that it needed it.

"What? Don't tell me you haven't written anything new yet."

"I'm just so distracted, you know?"

Lisa paused, "No, I don't."

"Got another letter. Thinking about going back."

"Oh, country girl can't handle the city, huh?"

"Girl, I can't keep living off of you. That's just not how I was raised. My people are proud people. We always had our own." Nora had begun living with Lisa just a few blocks from Spooner Street, just beyond the colored line where Jacobsville's colored middle class resided.

"Well, like I say, a lil struggle never hurt nobody. Just gotta stick with it. You know the SCC gonna be bailing tonight, right?" Nora laughed, remembering her first night at the Sugar Cane Club.

"Why you laughing? You need to come with me. You know its Thursday," danced Lisa.

"And?"

Lisa stopped and put her hands on her hips, "AND its free admission for women, don't act like you ain't know."

"You know that ain't even my scene."

"It needs to be. I bet you ain't even got you none yet, have you?"

Nora blushed, "You a mess!"

"Why I'm a mess? 'Cause I'm telling the truth? I know you ain't still a virgin. Are you?"

"I know that's none of your business."

"You mean to tell me you ain't hit nothing?

"I don't know nothing about no hitting," laughed Nora.

"You scared, huh?" Lisa returned to the stove. "I don't know why you don't like to have fun no more. You remember how we used to hang when you first got here."

Nora was silent. She remembered the fear that clung onto her that sizzling, blazing hot day at the Train Station. No family, and no place to go. The school money she stole from her parents didn't last long. Maybe Lisa was just in the right place at the right time. She became her saving grace, feeding her at first and then offering her a place on her sofa. Eventually, the two began hanging out, and Nora got used to the city. It was most exciting, but life got hard. There were no large lands to grow tomatoes on, or chickens running wild, whose heads you could chop off. Clothes were also store-bought, which was different for Nora. Back home Mama made the clothes, hand-washed them with lye soap, and then together they'd hang them outside to dry, using thick cords that ran from the large Oak Tree to the side of the house. The city didn't even have free lakes to swim in, and Nora wasn't used to buying meat and butter from the store. She remembered how Daddy slaughtered whole cows and they'd have food for a month of Sundays. It was up to her and Mama to churn the butter and bake the bread. She did miss hanging out with Lisa though, and the SCC was by far the hottest Jazz Club in Jacobsville.

"But you need to come with me tonight for real. You know Duke is in town."

"Yeah, I know."

"Nora!" Charlotte's scratchy voice held onto the last nerve Nora had left. Rolling her eyes, she marched on into the other room.

"Yes, Miss Charlotte?"

"It's Godmother to you."

"Godmother?" Nora's mouth twitched, *where'd this come*

from?

"Lisa!" shouted Charlotte as Lisa entered the room.

"From now on, I am Godmother."

"Why?"

"Because I am Lisa."

"Yes, Miss Charlotte we understand," said Lisa, silence filling the room. "Godmother Charlotte," she corrected.

"Nora hun, where's my coffee?"

"Right," murmured Nora, running into the kitchen. She came back with a tea cup sized glass and handed it to Charlotte with her head lowered and her hand extended.

"Raise that head child, this is the North."

Tell me about it. "Yes, ma'am," Nora tilted her head. It wasn't that she was afraid to look at her; she just hated to have to look into those eyes. Glassy. Empty. Miserable. "I mean, yes Godmother."

"It's cold," criticized Charlotte, as she stood, giving Nora back the cup and removing her night cap. Charlotte's reddish hair bounced around her face and glistened in the afternoon sun shining through the window. It was beautiful.

Lisa walked over to Charlotte's throne, taking her Mistress's hand as she lowered herself to the floor. Charlotte disposed of her night cap into Lisa's arms. "I'm going out," she announced, and Nora almost dropped the glass at what came next. Miss Charlotte was naked. She'd let her gown drop to her ankles as she stood there in the buff. Then she walked off and disappeared into the back room. Lisa gathered the belongings from off the floor.

CHAPTER THREE

ONE YEAR EARLIER
JUNE, 1922

"I'VE KNOWN RIVERS:
"I've known rivers ancient as the world and older than the
flow of human blood in human veins….
My soul has grown deep like the rivers."

NORA PAUSED, SMILING AT THE BABY BIRD occupying her
windowsill. It was high noon, but not sticky as usual. The way the
wind courted the white linen and the way they danced sent gallons
of fresh air rushing over her body like cool rain. She was happy with
herself to have finished the sheets in time for the wind to show off.
Mississippi air didn't feel good unless there was something clean to
go along with it to make it cool. Otherwise, it was warm air sucking
the life out your lungs; a stiff uneasy breeze like the scratchy fibers
of rope just waiting to wrap itself around someone's neck. The air

was like that in "Ole Miss", uncomfortably sitting above the earth. But not today. Today the sheets were white and clean and filled the air with a fresh breeze.

The bird chirped. He was the second one this afternoon. A dark streaked with brown and white down his sides, he was oddly identical to his friend. Nora waited for him to spread his wings wide like freedom quilts across the sky. Only then could she return to last month's issue of *The Crisis*. Not that she needed to. At a time where young women were scheming for secret hideouts in ways that left their womanhood dangling for the boys to latch onto, Nora locked herself away inside dreams made of brick walls.

"My soul has grown deep like the rivers.
I bathed in the Euphrates when dawns were young.
I built my hut near the Congo and it lulled me to sleep."

There were other favorites, but something about Langston's words in *The Negro Speaks of Rivers* set her soul aflame. She could smell the fresh air and feel the wetness of the waves between her toes. There was an ancient passion that shut themselves up in her bones whenever she read the poem, and she could not move or even breathe until after the moment had passed.

Nora lingered on the poem more so than the rest each day when she found time to slip away from the fields and spread her wings from one end of the room to the next. The bird flew away and Nora turned to the attention of the small wood dresser beside her. She carefully laid the paper to rest alongside the others, *The Opportunity*, and *Messenger,* before approaching the open window. She closed her eyes, breathing in what was left of the moment. When she opened them, there was no longer a stretch of dirt road and rows of peas or the sound of her parents yelling at her little brothers to go bathe.

When Nora opened her eyes, the sky was dark, the street lights replaced the sun, and the roads turned into the busy section of "The Black Mecca". Nora didn't need to visit Harlem to fall in love with it. On that windowsill, she stood in the crossfire of people and lights and cars and bobbed her head to the beat of ragtime syncopation and driving brass bands to soaring gospel choirs mixed with field hollers and the deep-down growl of the blues. Soon she was dressed in a peach dress and white blouse that illuminated the richness of her creamy brown skin, thick course hair, and brown eyes.

She danced to the groove of Fats Waller, Duke Ellington, Jelly Roll Morton, Willie "The Lion" Smith, Bessie Smith, Billie "Lady Day" Holiday, and Chick Webb. Legs swinging, roof rocking, neighbors knocking, and body incapable of standing still. Nora stood up on her toes and let her partner throw her over his back, let him throw her into the air again, and then slithered like her body was made of jellyfish underneath his legs. She danced as if she'd never had legs before, gliding and shaking in ways her father would never approve of. Nora flipped and split and cartwheeled around The Negro Club alongside Louis Jordan and The Nicholas Brother's until the sweat began to congregate alongside her forehead and trickle its way down to her chin.

"Nee-Nee!"

Just like that, it was over. The people scattered, the sky opened and the dirt roads reappeared along with the face of the world's most annoying little brother. Dream deferred.

"What?" Nora couldn't wait until she turned eighteen and could pursue her writing career on the first train smoking to New York, or so she hoped.

"Ain't you hot sitting out here in the sun?" Walter had noticed the water sliding down his big sister's face, and wiped his own with the shirt hanging outside of his overalls. It was filthy.

"Ain't you supposed to be in somebody's wash tub?"

Sunday night baths were the norm, but the boys got so dirty in the field that Mom was bathing them every night. Nora and Walter would take turns drawing the water up from the well on the land, Nora would set it to boil on the stove and let sit for cooling. Nobody wanted to hear the boys complain the water was too hot. They'd give any excuse not to get in. Then, Nora and Mother would haul the large round tub into the kitchen—the warmest room in the house—and fill it with the now warm water.

"Daddy want chu."

Nora rolled her eyes, "For what?"

"I dunno."

Nora blew a breath before rising from the windowsill. She knew what her father wanted. It was time to harvest the peas.

∗∗∗

Nora grabbed the sun hat from out of the closet and walked out into the living area where her thick black boots were overturned near the door. Mud caked the bottom and the shoe strings were dry and cracked from the last time she was in the fields.

"Ewww."

She used her thumb and index fingers to peel away the strings from inside the boot, and with great loathing, inserted her freshly painted toes into the darkness. It's been awhile since the ground was wet, and the dried mud churned Nora's stomach with every step.

Despite these feelings, however, Nora was well versed in her understanding of farming, having been raised in the education of the ground and its production of foods since she was Walter and Eddy's age. Approaching the garden bed, with Dad already bent over and humming to himself—he loved this way too much—Nora smiled as she pulled on the pink gloves and walked over to where the peas were.

"Hey babies."

Nora did not hate farming completely. She did love peas and took great pride in seeing the result of her labors. Southern peas were easy, productive, and delicious. The White family grew only the best varieties to include Mississippi Silver, Purple Hull, Whippoorwill, and Black-eyed. They grow on short vines and do not require fences; they like it relentlessly hot and humid; they weather droughts without blinking; and they grow in soil few other plants would survive in.

Nora began a hum of her own as she picked them, imagining sending Walter to the well for water and later cooking the peas in the heavy pot over a medium flame. They'll cook quickly to tender-yet-firm, their delicate flavor tasting of good soil and a hot sun. Other warm-weather foods The White's grew were spinach, peanuts, hot peppers, and sweet peppers. After an hour, Nora's patience ran thin.

"Whew, it's burning up out here," she complained, standing up straight and tilting her head toward the East where the sun was blazing. Except for tending to the peas, Nora preferred not to farm. Her parents had to work six days a week. It was rigorous, back-breaking work but farmers were working against the weather. When conditions were fair, you had to take advantage of it. When planting season was over, then it was growing season. She hated plunging the shovel into the dirt, pushing it with her foot and turning it over. Daddy called this "turning the ground over" and it could take hours depending on which part of the land Daddy wanted you to do. It was extra if you asked her. Freedom was supposed to mean sitting somewhere drinking lemonade, not working like a Hebrew slave. "Slavery again," she said under her breath. Gideon stood up, his tall body towering over Nora and the garden. Sweat drained from his head down to his cheeks. He pulled the handkerchief from his back pocket, mopped his forehead, and scanned the area.

"Take a look out yonder there."

"What?" said Nora, swatting at a bug.

Gideon extended his arm as if to indicate the land around them. The garden bed, trees, heads of cattle grazing by the fence that separated the White's land from the neighbors, chicken coop and the vibrant greenery of the family's five acres. It was beautiful the way the grass was always cut close to the ground.

"OK...," said Nora.

Gideon put the handkerchief back in his pocket and put his

hands on his hips.

"This here is what a man can do if he puts his mind to it and his back in it."

Nora rolled her eyes. *Here it comes.*

"Stop complaining. The world don't owe the colored man nothing. The colored man owes it to himself."

Nora wiped her face. Her father's voice was slow, calm, and serious. It was the beginning of a 15-minute lecture about the colored man. She hadn't meant for "slave" to come rolling off her tongue loud enough for him to hear.

"I know, Daddy."

"No, you don't know. I told you why we were slaves and how we ended up here in this land. Now the Almighty done planted us here and the least we can do is take advantage. You were born on this land. You can't change that and you can't change the past. All you can do is make the best of it. Nobody starves in my house, Nora. Do you want to know why nobody starves?"

Nora rolled her eyes again, she only heard this story fifty million times.

"Because of the land."

Gideon leaned his head forward and placed his hand over his ear, "I can't hear ya, what ya say now?"

"Because of the land!"

"Alright now, best get to it then."

CHAPTER FOUR

"AND DON'T BE ALL NIGHT WITH IT on account of Irene. That woman would talk you to tomorrow."

Nora waved her mother off and slung the sack over her shoulder as she left the house, relieved to be freshly bathed and in a change of clothes—her favorite sky-blue chiffon pleated mid skirt, white blouse, and sandals that freed her toes. She stopped, breathing in the air. Leaving the house was always something of an event. The 3,400 square feet, 5-bedroom home was a beauty. The house was built when her father was just a child, and was surrounded by beautiful trees to include Mr. Oak that sat in the middle of the land. Nora named the tree when she was just a girl because of the way it embraced her when she sat under it. It's thick branches bowing low, leaves hovering over her tiny body.

Nora began to walk, dreading the half mile journey to the General Store. It was where all the colored folk would go for goods, many of them paying with IOUs, running up tabs, and adding debt onto debt. They were tenant farmers, maids, and washerwomen. Negroes couldn't have guessed that the end of one form of servitude gave birth to another. Many of the families were the descendants of slaves whose ancestors had nothing more to look for in freedom but to be paid pennies to pick cotton. The White's were different, and their ownership of land, scarce. Only a few families owned their land despite General William T. Sherman's plan to grant freedmen 40 acres on the islands and coastal region of Georgia. After the Civil War, many colored folks were confident that with "40 Acres and a mule" they could work their own land after years of doing it for someone else. As Gideon taught his children, owning land was important and the source of economic stability and independence.

This, however, was not a reality for most families who were ordered to either sign contracts with the owners or be evicted, driven out by army troops. In the summer of 1865, all land had been ordered by the government to be returned to its original owners. As a result, millions of coloreds remained poor, spending most of their time doing what they've always done: picking cotton on the same plantations that held them as slaves.

"Hey there!"

Irene's voice leaped from her front porch and met Nora down the road.

"Hey Miss Irene."

"Now why you standing all the way over there? Come on over let me talk to ya. Ain't seen much of you lately. Not since that fine graduation party your folks put on."

The wind blew dust into the air, and Nora watched as if it was something of interest. Her heart sank and the blood rushed underneath her skin. She didn't have time for this. Miss Irene never left her front porch for fear she'd miss something. Did Sara put Donald out the house again? Was the Collins boy stealing money out his mother's purse in the night? Miss Irene probably slept with one eye open, watching the boy's shadow move about the open curtains. And what of that May girl? She knocked up once more? Indeed, the front porch was the best place to be for Miss. Irene to keep up with everyone's business. She dared not move a muscle.

Irene was a nice old woman, but didn't know how to shut up. Of course, those weren't words Nora could say out loud, especially not to a nice old lady. *Shut up* was a curse word, and besides, children were on strict command to stay in their place. She wasn't exactly a child anymore, but apparently, her mother and the rest of the town didn't know it yet. Not when her hips spread out and her breasts came in. Not when Molly celebrated the start of her cycle like it was her birthday, and not even when she graduated from High School. Nope. Nora White was still the little colored girl running around with pigtails.

She trudged forward, dragging her feet through the red dirt covered road. It wouldn't be so bad if Irene wanted something.

"How ya mama doing?"

"She doing good Miss Irene."

"Good, that's good."

Irene went on rocking the old wood chair.

"You decided where you wanna go? I'm just so excited for you. Always knew Molly's girl was gonna make it."

Here we go again. She wished everyone would stop asking her that.

"I haven't decided yet." Nora directed her attention across the road. A group of children were playing tag. Her eyes landed on the boys and her lips curled up in adoration. Her little brothers were everything.

"You better hurry up child, summer's almost over."

"I know, Miss Irene. Imma make a decision soon."

"That's sho nuff fine. We need more youngins lak yourself doing something with they life."

"Well, Miss Irene I better get going. Gotta hurry on back for dinner. You know how Mama worries."

"OK, well hold on there, baby, let me get my list. I'm shole glad you here."

Nora blew a breath. This is why she hated walking to the store. Not only did she have to shop for her house, but for everybody else's on the way. She usually enjoyed it, but since graduation she'd been in an impatient mood and wished everyone would shut up already about college this and university that.

Irene grabbed the walking stick leaning against the house and rose to her feet with the slowness of a woman with infinite time on her hands.

"Whew, child. Yea you gone and exercise them young legs ya got. You'll need 'em when you my age." Irene chuckled and crawled on into the house.

***

As soon as Nora turned the corner the voices greeted her, rising into the air like thick smoke and invading her ears. As expected, the front porch of the store was jam packed with people, and most of them not buying customers. The checker boards were out and all the chairs were occupied. Men smoked their pipes and drank their beers and ice-cold Coca-Cola's, gambling away their earnings and complaining about it later. There were also a few women sprinkled about who saw no fun in washing clothes and feeding husbands. They were what Mother referred to as loose, and Nora was warned to stay away from them. "They ain't got nothing better to do but try and take somebody else's man." Molly's voice was bitter to Nora's ears, and she wondered if Mom's words had to do with a personal encounter.

The store carried an assortment of toys: jacks, marbles, yo-yo's, tops, pick-up sticks, and local Mississippi products, including Mississippi Bees Honey, Pennington Farms Honey, Hillside Vineyards Jelly and Jams, Mississippi Cheese Straws, and even fabric. It wasn't just a place of shopping, it was also a time to hang out and forget—if only for a moment—what the next day had in store.

Nora started for the back, hoping to avoid the crowd.

"Nee-Nee! Nee-Nee, that you?"

Of course, it was an unlikely goal.

"Hey John, Betty, Paul, Helen, Dorothy, everybody."

The porch laughed as Nora walked up. She felt uneasy. Everyone was looking at her. The world stopped and waited. At least it felt like it.

"So, let's hear it," Helen leaned against the pole on the porch with her arms folded, tapping her firecracker red high heeled shoes—the same color as her lipstick—against the weak porch. She was Thomas' wife, even if she was here with John, but that was none of Nora's business.

"Hear what?"

"She tryna be shy now y'all," Helen waved Nora off and took a seat next to John.

"Well she got a right to be what she wants," said Paul, "I'm on my way to College myself."

"What?" John turned up his lip, "negro, you can't even read!"

The porch laughed.

"How you know what I can do? I been reading since befo you been alive, young man."

"And you out here picking cotton lak the rest of us."

The porch laughed again and Nora cracked a smile, remembering the first time she learned to read. Dad made sure all his children was reading by the time they were three, and his and Mama's stories of the olden days made Nora eager for her lesson. She'd spend hours under the tree reading until the urge to create stories in her head tugged at her like an empty stomach in need of food.

Nora tried to squeeze by two men engaged in a game of checkers.

"How ya mama doing? Tell her I can use a hand on the old stitch," said Dorothy.

Dangit. "I will."

"What she up to anyway? Ya mama?" said Betty.

"Oh, she's doing good."

"Yea," spoke one of the men, without looking up from his game. "I remember Molly when she was 'bout yo age."

The porch joined in, agreeing in murmurs.

"That when she first come here with your father, ya see. Wasn't nothing but a lil ole thang. They shole was in love too, you could tell. Before you know it, they was moved into that place of Clara's up yonder and you was on the way."

"That's the White's for you. Always on the up and up," said Helen.

"I can only imagine what I'd do if I owned that kinda land. Y'all still got those Walnut trees on up there? Ya mama selling peaches this year?" said John.

"She don't know yet. Don't have Walnut trees that I know of. Just peaches and apple."

Nora's heart raced. People were jealous of her family, and she didn't know if they were truly interested or just being funny. Besides, what's so special about land anyway? Who wanted to spend the free time they had in the sun all day? Her family had a little something, but they weren't rich like people thought.

"I always knew she was gonna be something too," said Paul.

"Who that?" said one of the men.

"The girl's mama."

"Oh yea," said the man, "most definitely. She was a smart one there. Ole Gideon lucked up on that one."

"Or she lucked up on him," Helen and Betty slapped hands, laughing.

"Especially married to a White. That erase the curse fa sho," said a man who hadn't spoken before. He chuckled at his own joke.

Nora's face felt hot, "What do you mean?"

The porch looked at Nora like she had three eyeballs and then at the man who'd spoken. Someone let the cat out the bag.

"Now ain't you no fool? Can't hold hot water," said Dorothy.

"Hell," said John, "he can't hold cold water."

"Don't matter what kind of water it is, Frank can't hold it." The porch burst into a thunderous laughter before quieting again, and Nora marked Frank in her mind.

"Frank, what do you mean *erase the curse?*"

"Oh baby, he don't even know. Making up stuff as he goes along, ole fool," said Dorothy.

"Yea, gone on in there and take care ya hog killing. He ain't mean nothing by it baby. The man always talking out the side of his neck, don't know what he say half the time. That's what happens you get up there in age," said Paul.

Nora turned to walk away, forcing herself away from the porch and into the solace of the coolness of the store. She needed to feel the fresh air on her skin and in her lungs. What did Frank mean *"erase the curse?"*

CHAPTER FIVE

"I DON'T KNOW MOLLY, I think Nee-Nee catchin' up to ya," laughed Gideon as he scrapped the last bit of peach cobbler from his plate.

"Nee-Nee ain't lived long enough to catch up to me," laughed Molly, as Nora and her father exchanged looks and snickered among themselves.

"Speaking of catching up, have you decided what school you gonna be attending now, child? Fisk or Tuskegee? Or have your father already talked you into staying local?"

Molly White laughed and bent her back, grimacing at the pain. Years of hard work had begun the slow process of catching up to her. Molly was a thick-boned woman and shaped like a Coca-Cola bottle: flat stomach, wide hips, plump behind, and melon-sized breasts. Her skin was Russet, like dark brown with a reddish tinge;

her hair long, brown and silky. But Molly had a voice that didn't fit her body. Instead of soft and delicate, it was strong and authoritative, booming from deep inside her throat and commanding the attention of the room. Molly was a lively woman who feared nobody except her man and dared anyone to challenge it. It was no wonder Gideon mean mugged every man on the street. "Why you look so mean for?" Molly would ask in the early years. "Because," said Gideon, "just in case."

Nora lowered her head and wondered why the room grew silent. She wished Eddy would make a loud noise or something to release the tension burning a hole in her skin. The four-year-old had a hard time coming into the world, and they almost lost him. He was their parent's baby, their most prized possession.

"I don't wanna go to College."

Gideon cleared his throat, "Walter, gone take this plate on over to the sink, then grab your brother and y'all gone and start your reading."

"But Dad—" complained Walter.

"Gone do what I say now," interrupted Gideon, who watched the boys like a hulk until they were out of the room. He noticed that Molly had not released her stare from Nora's face.

"And when did you decide all of this?" It was difficult to tell when Gideon was angry; he spoke low, his breath controlled, his eyes focused. Nora fidgeted with her spoon and tried to scoop up what tiny crumbs remained on the plate before Molly grabbed the dish, a silent demand of an answer as she held it in her hands.

"I think your father asked you a question, young lady." Molly was the opposite of her husband. Nora's heart skipped a beat.

Mom was definitely angry.

"And unfold those arms," said Gideon.

Gideon was a tall man whose voice was calm and yet held an authority that stopped you from breathing. Gideon, also known as "Dee", was a dark-skinned man like the night sky with big bulging eyeballs and thick lips, a wide nose and hands that were huge and scarred. There were rumors about those hands. Rumors that they'd done terrible things, like crushed the skulls of the white men who murdered his sister long ago. After the men went missing, they say Gideon wore a smirk on his face that made his mother tremble in her bones. No one would ever know if the rumors were true, but no one would ever dare to ask him about it either.

Nora scanned the house, focusing her attention on the front door which she could see from the kitchen table. Due to Eddy and Walter, it was always left hanging open. This was fine with everyone in the house, as it let in a cool breeze.

"Nora, you hear me talking to you?"

Molly's voice caused Nora's heart to skip again, "Yes ma'am. I know that it's important and everything, but I feel like this is your dream, not mine."

Molly slammed the plate down on the table with enough force to express her anger, but not enough to break it. If there was one thing Molly treasured, it was her dishes. Cutting her eyes at Dee, she calmed herself and sat in one of the chairs at the table.

"Then what is your dream then, Nora? You may be good at it, but writers don't make money, honey. And what are you gonna do? Help your father and me work this land for the rest of your life?"

"No, Mom."

"Then what is it then? 'Cause in case you ain't noticed, there ain't much available out here for us colored folk, and yet here you are, blessed. Sitting in a house twice the size of your neighbors and eating food you planted yourself, but you don't care about that, huh? About your ancestors who worked hard to give us what we have here today."

"What your mother's trying to say is that you need a plan, sweetheart. What are your plans?"

"I was hoping to go to New York and get published and—"

"—I know this better not be about that Harlem Renaissance mess! That place is crawling with white folk through and through," interrupted Molly.

Last year, the Greenwood neighborhood of North Tulsa was systematically bombed and destroyed by the Klan. One of the most successful and wealthiest Negro communities in the United States burned down to the ground, leaving over 800 people admitted to local hospitals and thousands of Negroes—millionaires who had been the owners of brick houses and multiple businesses— homeless and destitute.

At the end of the day, June 1, 1921, only piles of dirt, gravel, empty shells of buildings and dead bodies remained of Black Wall Street. Lost forever were over 600 successful businesses, including 21 restaurants, 30 grocery stores, two movie theaters, a hospital, a bank, a post office, libraries, schools, law offices, a half dozen private airplanes, and a bus system. But this was only the most recent calamity.

The year before that, on October 5, 1920, four Negro men were killed in MacClenny, Florida, following the death of a prominent white farmer named John Harvey. According to news reports, Harvey was shot and killed at a turpentine camp near MacClenny on October 4, 1920. The suspected shooter, a young Negro man named Jim Givens, fled immediately afterward, and mobs of armed white men formed to pursue him. Givens's brother and two other colored men connected to him were questioned and jailed during the search, though there was no evidence or accusation that they had been involved in the killing of Harvey. A shiver ran down Molly's spine. It was enough to keep her as far away from anything that will upset the status quo or angry white folk in general. Especially considering what happened to Gideon's sister.

"With what money?" said Gideon.

"Well, I was hoping to use my school money."

"The money we worked for? That money? The money we been out there slaving for so you can get on and do something with your life? The money from the land you hate so much? Have you lost your mind?" Molly's hands trembled and her knees bounced up and down.

"And when that money runs out, then what?" Gideon didn't wait for an answer. "And where would you stay? And with whom? Do you know of anyone out there? Who's going to look out for you? These are questions that need answers Nee-Nee. You can't just jump up and go places because you read about it in some paper."

"It's not just any place!"

"Watch your tone," said Gideon.

Nora calmed, "Mom, Dad, this is what I wanna do. I want to write and be published and speak on behalf of my people. If I go to college, it will make you happy. But will I be happy there?"

"Don't play that reverse stuff with me, girl! It's not about being happy; it's about being smart! And going all the way up there with no money and no family just ain't smart. I don't care what you say."

Molly rose from her seat and began to clear the table. It was a sign that she was done talking and had made up her mind. Tears welled and broke slowly from Nora's eyes.

"Molly calm down now. But Nee-Nee, your mother's right. If you really wanna go somewhere, you need to have a plan first. That's what this family has been built on. We always had our own because we were willing to work toward it. We ain't stomping on your dreams now, but it doesn't sound like ya really know what you doing and what ya want." Gideon rose from the table, and placed a hand on Nora's trembling shoulder. It was warm and Nora felt five all over again. He patted twice and then walked out the room. Nora sat there a moment as her mother moved about, mumbling her discontent.

"Talking 'bout some happy. You get to where you can feed your family, have some kind of dignity and pride about yourself. It's what your dad's parents did and it is what our ancestors did. The White's ain't worried none about being happy. You get to where you have a roof over your head and food in your stomach. Then you can concern yourself with the likes of being happy."

"May I be excused?" Nora barely got the words out. She was boiling over with the desire to write. What she wanted to write she didn't know, but the anger was more than enough fuel to get her wheels turning.

"Gone get on outta my face, child," waved Molly.

CHAPTER SIX

MOLLY BUSIED HERSELF IN THE BEDROOM, her mind still racing with thoughts of Nora. Where'd she go wrong? She tried to pin point the exact moment her parenting skills faltered. Is it because she never really had parents of her own? Molly's eyebrows carved deep lines in her forehead at the thought as she slammed the bureau shut.

"You know that girl been out there almost an hour?" Gideon blew a breath. He was already in bed with his underwear on, white T-shirt, and face toward the ceiling; it was covered with his hat. *When was she going to turn the lights off?*

"You really need to calm down now. The girl just being herself is all."

"You think maybe she's imagining—"

"No," interrupted Gideon. He didn't want to contemplate the implications of Molly's question.

Molly grunted, "Hmmm, I bet she done met somebody. Dee, you reckon she met somebody? I bet she did sho nuff."

Gideon threw the hat across the room and watched it land on the floor. He'll pick it up later.

"What I reckon is that pretty soon that light's gonna go off and you gonna hop on over here witcha man. I know you're worried, but you know how the young ones get at this age; they think they knows it all."

"I bet she been getting into that drinking mess too, with them lil fast tail girls on down at the church. Lil heifer."

"If I know one thing about baby girl, is that baby girl ain't into that drinking. She can't anyway."

"See now there you go."

"There I go what, woman?"

"There you go taking up for her. Same as always. She ain't gonna never learn if you keep coddling her like you do."

Gideon chuckled, "Well see that's the problem. Ain't enough colored girls being coddled as is."

"I'm serious, Dee."

"Hell, I'm serious too. She the only daughter I got. You telling me I can't spoil her?"

Molly slipped in her night gown and sat on the bed.

"This ain't about spoiling your daughter; this is about you taking her side every time I'm trying to chastise her."

Gideon ignored his wife and moved closer, wrapping his big black arms around her waist and firmly palming her booty.

"Looks like I'm on yo side," he said smiling and burying his face into Molly's neck. His mustache sent warm chills down her spine.

She couldn't help but to smile.

"Don't try and change the subject, Dee."

"I ain't changing the subject. We were talking about whose side I'm on."

Molly laughed, "Umm, your sons are still awake in the other room and your daughter is still outside acting like she done lost her puppy."

"Maybe she did."

The lines in Molly's forehead curled. Gideon sat up in the bed.

"Alright woman. I'll go see about her. Don't you go nowhere now."

"Where Imma go, Dee?"

"I don't know, just don't."

Molly smiled, watching her husband slip into his pants and T-Shirt before exiting the room. He was still the most sexiest man she'd ever met. The curtains shifted in the breeze. It was a beautiful night out. The crickets sang, the frogs cried out, and the wind whistled. The calming tune mesmerized Molly and convinced her to slip back into memories of her young life. She thought she'd done well. Nora was a smart girl and had made it through High School without getting pregnant or running off with some "no count nigga", as her grandmother used to say. She hated to think some young fool done got in her head and filled it with all kinds of dreams that would never come true. Grandma Susie warned her of such things, *"Or you gonna be jest like ya no count Mammy"*.

✳✳✳

Grandma never said much about Mom. Not what she liked, disliked, nothing. It was as if to Molly that her mother never really existed; just a figment of her grandmother's mind, someone to complain about. Strict and high on discipline, Grandma Susie was sure to keep Molly as secluded as possible. *"Or ya gonna mess around and be jest like her."* Molly didn't understand Grandma, what she meant, or why she was so angry and mean all the time. At times Molly felt alone, like she was living with a stranger. No mama. No daddy. No sisters and brothers, and no grandmother either.

"You alright, Grandma?"

"Yes, I'm alright! Hell you mean am I alright? You finish those dishes lak I say?"

"Yes, Grandmother."

"What did you call me?"

"I—I said yes," stammered Molly.

"Yes...who?"

"Yes, Grandmother."

Before Molly knew it, Susie had a back hand coming her way. She never did hit her, but the gesture was a threatening one that sent Molly scurrying away and Grandma following her with words of shame and ridicule. Grandma Susie didn't like to be called Mommy or Grandmother. It was the Mother part, and Mommy especially, that had her going. A rage surfaced like something Molly had never seen. A bitterness that even in her own mouth tasted like stale coffee. Something was left over in Grandmother's soul and had begun to rot. She thought maybe Grandma was just sick. She was old, after all, and grew up a slave. *Maybe she's having flashbacks,* thought Molly.

Molly's life consisted of chores, school, and taking care of Grandmother. There wasn't much time for socializing outside of Sunday church. Molly didn't understand church either. *"How could Grandmamma be so mean at home and so loving at church?"* There was something special about Sundays, though, that made Molly grow fond of them. It began during weekend revival and the Pastors in Training Program, when young reverends in training traveled with their mentors to see if they could work a crowd. It was the first-time young Pastor Kenneth Johnson visited with his *fine* cousin.

With him were members of his small church back home and the darkest black she's ever seen. He was tall with large hands, lips like pillows, and eyes that watched her from across the room. Those eyes. They seemed to look right through her very soul. Molly wiggled in her seat and pretended to focus so that Grandmother's words wouldn't punch her when they got home—storming into her bedroom and slapping against her self-esteem for no reason at all. He made it hard though. That dark figure of a man with the piercing eyes. She wished he'd look away, his presence made her uncomfortable. That warmness that crept over her body and shooting right down to her private parts. Molly found herself getting upset. No one deserved to have their privacy invaded like that.

"Is there something you want?"

Exhausted victims of the Holy Ghost migrated to the kitchen for lunch before the start of evening service. It was just the beginning of a very long day to an even longer week. Grown-ups gossiped to pass the time in the oppressive heat, waving paper fans back and forth while children dragged their feet and babies whined on their mother's hips; the frustration of hunger setting in. The line stretched long down the hall. It was the perfect occasion to approach the stalker of her soul while Grandmama was somewhere being saved.

"Excuse me?" said those eyes. His voice was calm, intelligent, strong.

"Stop looking at me," Molly's eyebrows rose and her mouth twitched, but *Eyes* could tell it was a farce. He smiled.

"You came all the way over here to tell me that?"

The red raced to Molly's cheeks, "Well I just thought I'd say it's probably not a good idea for you to be stalking people in God's house."

The boy smirked, "Is that right?"

"Yup," Molly's hands were on her hips, and those eyes roamed her body. She cleared her throat.

"See? You're doing it again. Stop looking at me like that."

"I'm the stalker but you came over here—"

The boy looked down the line toward the end where Ms. Locklear stood talking to an elderly woman.

"—to talk to me?"

There it is again. She was usually good at telling off boys. She'd better walk away before making a complete fool of herself.

"Wait, what's your name? You do have one, right?"

"I don't just be giving my name over to strangers you know."

Eyes held out his hand and Molly's heart pounded.

"Dee."

"Your mother named you a letter?" Molly folded her arms across her chest.

"Gideon, but everybody calls me Dee. Besides, my father named me."

She took the hand in hers and a shiver ran down her body. Hopefully he didn't notice the goosebumps on her skin. His one hand swallowed hers. It felt as if she had just stuck it in an oven and the heat traveled from her hands and crawled its way through her body. Gideon smiled, his dreams of touching the pretty Indian-looking girl in the church pews had finally come true, and her skin (milk brown and smooth) felt better than silk against his. He tried to remember if he'd ever touched a girl's skin that soft.

"Molly Davis. As you can see, I have a last name too."

"You're beautiful."

Molly blushed again, "What?"

"I said you're beautiful."

Molly cut her eyes seductively, walking away with certainty that her newly arrived hips and the way her plump backside filled out her dress caused that Dee boy to take another look. The way her cheeks jiggled like jelly over the thin spread of the fabric, she was sure of it. Molly walked away as if she owned the world, like butterflies weren't fluttering about in her stomach. That was the beginning of Molly and Gideon. The visits became more abundant. Molly never knew how much Gideon hated church and only insisted his cousin "sharpen his preaching skills" by visiting so he can watch her. Eventually, Gideon found his own excuse to visit and found out just how soft Molly's skin was.

Of course, they had to keep this love affair secret, for

Grandma Susie was insistent that Molly would not turn out like her mother. The statement only bothered Molly because she didn't know her mother. It was irritating and made her feel shame, a constant reminder that she was no one's daughter. If there was anyone in the world she should resemble, Grandmother made sure to insist it should not be her mother. *Fine with me,* Molly would think. There were no memories of her anyway. Well, there were almost no memories.

Molly had forgotten all about Gideon and lost herself in daydreams. Absently, she licked her lips. She could still taste the chocolate that oozed into her mouth, and the sound of her mother's voice that sent the cookie slipping from her fingers.

CHAPTER SEVEN

1889

"NOW HOLD ON ONE MINUTE NOW."

Susie sat up and reached for the double barrel shotgun leaning against the closet door as the front door thundered from the other room. Pulling the curtains back, the window to the two-bedroom shack gave perfect view of the front porch and the figure bobbing back and forth and peering into the window. Susie's heart fluttered and her blood raced.

"What the hell?" Susie put the gun back, swung her feet off the bed, stood up, and started toward the door as it thundered once more.

"Alright. I said I'm coming!"

What was her nineteen-year-old daughter doing knocking her

door down in the middle of the night? Susie reached for the knob and took a deep breath before the thunder came again, almost knocking her back. She slung the door open.

"Girl! Have you lost yo damn mind! You tryna kill me, heifer?"

The woman's eyes darted around like ping pong balls looking for somewhere to land, and her jet-black hair hung down to her waist. Susie's Massa had been an Indian man of the Cherokee Tribe, and their daughter took on most of his features; a beautiful woman who right now did not look at all like herself. Her eyes were glossy and empty in the darkness as her hands kept still behind her back.

"What are you doing here Maxine?" Confusion washed into Susie's eyes as she stared her only child in the face.

"I can't do it, Mama," Maxine stammered as she continued to look around. Susie smelled liquor on her breath and released the defense mechanism a mother's heart had tried to keep back.

"Oh, no you will not. Not today. I don't know what you gonna do, but you gonna have to find somewhere else to go to do it, I got no time for your—"

Maxine's body wiggled back and forth as her arms struggled to keep still behind her back.

"And what in heaven's name are you doing?"

"Mama I need your help, I—"

"Did you not just hear what I said? I'm not going to keep putting up with this, Maxine, while you run ya fast self down over there with them bootleggers and gamblers and carrying on. Now I done sent you over ways to Uncle Bob and he supposed to be looking out for you but, obviously, he ain't doing his job."

"Fine, I don't need your help."

"See there, that's what I'm talking about. Don't neva know what it is you want."

"Mommy. Who are you talking to, Mom?"

Susie was so busy scolding Maxine that she didn't notice anyone else on the porch. No wonder Maxine moved around so much.

Maxine bent down to see the girl face to face, and Susie's hands covered her mouth. Maxine smiled weakly, running her hands over the girl's silky hair. It took on her volume, but without the color. Instead of black like hers, it was brown like her father's, with a reddish tinge. Maxine held onto the smile as she cupped the little girls face in her hands. She tried fighting the painful quiver in her throat, the one that burned if it wasn't released soon to match the tears in her eyes. She looked up to Mother Susie and the water broke, cascading down her cheeks.

"This is Susie. Grandma Susie. She's the one I've been telling you about. She's going to take good care of you."

"Mommy, why are you crying?" The little girl ignored the strange older lady standing in the doorway with her hand over her chest and tears in her eyes.

"Because, sweetie, I just love you so much."

Maxine took the girl in her arms and hugged her tight.

"I love you too, Mommy," said the girl as Maxine forced herself to pull away and stood up, holding her daughter's hand.

Susie couldn't stop staring at the little girl, a miniature version of her mother. She even had the long eyelashes. *Grandmother?*

"Mama, this is Margaret—"

"Lattice Davis!" interrupted the girl.

Maxine smiled big, "Good Job!"

Susie stood speechless. She couldn't take her eyes off little Margaret, and neither could her heart.

"Davis after her father," Maxine said quickly to give reason why the girl didn't carry her mother's stupid last name.

"But we call her—"

"Molly!" shouted Margaret.

"Good!" said Maxine, "and Molly is..."

"Three years old. Molly is three years old."

Susie found a smile and allowed it room on her face.

"And Molly, this is Grandma Susie."

"Hi, Susie," said the tiny voice.

"Grandma Susie," Maxine corrected.

"Hi, Grandma Susie. Can we go now, Mom?"

The smile on Susie's face disappeared and as Molly thought back, perhaps that is the last she's seen it. The wind seemed to notice, picking up gust and rattling Molly's small frame. She began to shiver.

"Why are you doing this?" said Susie, taking the girl's hand and ushering her into the house. Maxine folded her arms and watched as her mother sat Molly at the table—something in her stirred. She looked over the aged piece of furniture, dark brown with faded color legs. She focused on the legs, counting the scratch marks at the bottom. Her heart sank. She remembered depending on that table. Amazing how certain situations were so dire that it caused one to trust, even in a table. Maxine looked away. It had, after all, betrayed her. She held onto it for dear life, her body sprawled on the floor, fingers clutched onto the leg, and it did nothing to relieve her of the pain. Such severe and agonizing pain. A breeze blew and the goosebumps grew on top Maxine's skin, and her heart welcomed the cold.

"It ain't gonna do that child no good punishing me," Susie spoke low, closing the door to a crack.

"Punishing you? Oh, no, Mother. I'm not punishing you. I'm rewarding you." The liquor danced on Maxine's lips and gave her the courage she never had to face her mother head on. Susie raised her hands in the air and brought them back down on her face.

"Mercy!"

"Who are you talking to? God? Oh, well, I don't think he's listening," said Maxine.

"What is the matter with you, child?" Susie's voice trembled and cracked.

"Mom!" yelled Molly, but the women ignored her.

"Oh, are we playing that game again? The part where you tell the church I went crazy to save face? Oh, that's right!" Maxine threw her head back with a giggle.

"Leave. Leave this house right now."

"Yes, there it is. That's what I was looking for. You know that aching pain you're feeling right now? That agonizing guilt? I felt that once. In this very house in fact."

The tears gushed from Susie's eyes, "I don't want to hear it Maxine, why won't you just leave? Just go!"

"You don't want to hear it, huh? Truth don't sound good when it's brought to your face, now does it? How you tied me up..."

"Stop it Maxine," stammered Susie.

"—and spread my legs..."

"Maxine Locklear!"

"Can we go home now, Mom?" Molly's voice inside the house made Susie jump and look back. She marveled at how smart the child was. Secretly, she was proud that Maxine had obviously got her some learning since Susie herself never did learn to read.

"—and took my baby from me..." Maxine broke down. The courage subsided and was replaced with tears that took her to her knees, and her entire body trembled. In that moment, she had become a child again and Susie let the tears fall as she watched her daughter bend over, howling like she didn't have a care in the world.

"Mommy!" Molly's voice cried from inside the house.

"Yes, Mommy!" cried Maxine.

"Stop it now. Out here making a fool of yaself!" yelled Susie.

"Mom!" Molly was crying now.

"Yes baby, call her. Mommy! Mommy! Mommy!" Yelled Maxine. She was hysterical. She felt the rage consume her, and the mixture of alcohol and pain was too much energy to contain. Leaving her mother's porch, she ran around in circles on the front lawn.

"Mommy! Mommy!" cried Maxine, extending both her arms in the wind. They were wings and she was free.

"Mom!" Molly had climbed down from her seat and ran toward the door. As she was crying, she struggled to get past Grandma Susie, whose hips were too much for her tiny hands.

"Can't you hear her, Mother? She wants you. Your daughter wants you."

Susie turned away from the stranger running around in circles and scooped a crying Molly into her arms.

"No. I want Mom." The little girl was stronger than Susie thought, fighting and kicking to get toward the door.

"Its OK, baby!" shouted Maxine, "You're home now! You're home!"

"Mommy!" screamed Molly as Susie slammed the door shut.

"Yes. Call her. Mommy," Maxine's voice was now distant from behind the door. Susie wrestled a fighting Molly into her arms, rocking her on the chair she once used to rock her mother. The noise stopped and Susie was still. She'd given up trying to tame Molly and let her run to the door. Finding it locked, she slid to the floor and continued to cry until she fell into an exhausted slumber.

"I can still feel him inside of me."

Susie jumped, Maxine's voice was startling. It was close. She had to be standing right behind the door.

"My baby. The one you took from me. And God! Your precious sweet Jesus just sat back and watched," laughed Maxine.

"You was nothing but a baby yaself!" Susie had had enough.

"That's alright, Mommy," said Maxine in a child-like voice. "You can have this one too."

***

Susie had regrets, but what could she do with a pregnant twelve-year-old barely out of slavery? It happened too much then, and she'd vowed that she would not carry a slave's tradition to freedom. Far as she was concerned, that was slavery. What could she do as a mother? Besides, slavery had provided all the skills she needed to do it herself. Massa Salal LockLear always had women on the plantation "loosing youngins" in pregnancy and heck; he just figures something wrong with the nigga genes. Susie chuckled to herself. "Nigga Genes".

"That what he calls 'em, sho nuff," she said out loud, speaking to the air.

"It ain't my fault. No, it ain't," Susie spoke into the silence. "What was I supposed to do? Huh? Twelve years old. Humph. I knew how to do it. Done seen it my whole life hows to do it."

Susie smiled, "I knew what plant she needed, which ones was safe, and how long to boil the root and how much to take to stop it." Susie rocked back and forth.

"Hmm, yep. Sure did now. And I stopped it!" The house echoed, and Susie went on. "That baby wasn't yours. Wasn't gonna be. You hear me?"

Susie was silent a moment, her eyes falling on Molly, sleep on the floor.

"So, what was I to do but take it? Yea, she right. I took it. I'm the bad guy. But you know what? It saved her life. Sure nuff did. Saved the slave woman's life so's they ain't have no more product for Massa to gone and sell off. Making new product for Massa to sell, how that sound? So yea, I did it. I killed her baby and it saved her life." Susie listened for the sound of Maxine's voice behind the door.

It never came.

CHAPTER EIGHT

"MOM."

Molly broke from her daydream at the sound of Walters voice.

"You're crying."

Molly looked down at the boy; she hadn't noticed the stream of tears on her own face. She wiped them away.

"Get on up here," she said, patting the bed as Walter jumped in.

He couldn't help the giggles. Maybe he'll get to sleep here tonight! Ever since Eddy came along and he was old enough to have his own bed, his parent's room had been off limits. Times they were allowed was like being invited to a secret club. First, they had to bathe, and then Mom checked your feet to make sure they were clean. Then she checked with Dad to make sure it was alright, and when he gave the nod, you were lifted like a prince into the secret chamber. The covers were always huge, soft and clean, and if Dad was in a good mood, he'll tell you all kinds of stories while Mama rocked you to sleep. *Wait till I tell Lil Man I got to sleep with Mom and Dad!*

"So, tell me, how was your—"

"Walter get down, go see about your brother." Gideon stormed through the house and into the bedroom.

"But Dad, Eddy's—" whined Walter.

"Do it now."

Molly was disturbed at Dee's demeanor as Walter climbed down from the bed and complained on out of the room.

"Dee, what's wrong?"

Gideon ignored her, rushing toward the tall wood cabinet and searching around. Molly knew what for. She held her hand over her chest and rushed out the bed.

"Dee, what's wrong?" There was a quiver in her voice, a sign that she knew exactly what was wrong. It was a question she did not have to ask, for a mother's instinct had already revealed it, like an umbilical cord connecting her still to her child.

"Where's Nora?"

Gideon found the gun and cocked it back, storming toward the bedroom door.

"Dee!" Molly yelled after her husband, slipping on a pair of pants and a shirt that was too long to be hers. "Dee! Wait for me!" she yelled, as his footsteps echoed throughout the house. Molly made it to the front door where her sons were already watching in their pajamas.

"Mom, where's Dad?" said Eddy.

"Walter, watch your brother," the boys watched as Molly ran

out to catch up with Gideon.

Walter folded his arms and pouted. He was tired of this. Ever since Eddy came along, there was no more room for him. *Watch your brother, read to your brother, help your brother.* So what he was oldest, it was only by two years anyway. The six-year-old frowned. "Come on man."

"I want Mom," said Eddy. He was tired of being bossed around by Walter.

"I said c'mon!" yelled Walter, pulling Eddy over to the sofa.

"Sit there and don't move."

"Where you goin?" said Eddy.

"I'm going to get Dad."

"Me too!"

"No. Just sit. Imma be back."

"I'm telling."

"No, you're not," said Walter.

"Mommy!"

Walter slapped his hand against Eddy's mouth. Eddy bit Walter's finger.

"Owe!"

Eddy took the chance to run toward the door, but his little feet were too slow for big brother. Walter ran toward Edward and dragged him back to the couch.

***

"Dee?"

Molly folded her arms across Gideon's shirt that wrapped

around her upper body. The wind blew strong and there was a chill in the Mississippi air. Running, she caught up to him.

"Damn," said Gideon, holding the gun in his hands and fighting back tears.

"Where is she, Dee?" Flashbacks of her sister-in-law's disappearance cascaded through her mind, and the tears fell. It was her fault. Dee was right; she shouldn't have been so hard on her.

"I don't know," said Gideon, running.

"Dee, wait."

Molly ran behind Gideon until they approached a small house with steps and a rocking chair on the front porch. Pots and pans hung on the old vinyl and a light swung on the old farm door; it was on. *Good*, thought Gideon. That meant Charles was home. Gideon knocked against the door, tapping at first. He didn't know if Pearl was sleeping. Molly sat in the chair and folded her arms across her chest. Gideon knocked again, this time with urgency. A man approached the door smoking a pipe.

"Hey there!" Charles smiled big and grabbed the cowboy hat he didn't need from someplace close in the house and stepped outside the door. His boots slammed hard into the weak porch and one of the straps on his overalls hung off. Charles was more country than any of their friends and had known Gideon since they were boys.

"Now what do I owe the company of you fine people?" Charles chuckled as Molly stood to greet him.

"Molly Wolly," he said holding the pipe between his lips and engulfing her into his arms.

Charles' eyes were always just a little glossy than usual

because Charles was always just a little drunk. He pulled Molly back from his chest. That is when he saw her tear-streaked cheeks, Gideon's demeanor, and the gun. He let Molly go and took the pipe out of his mouth.

"Well, I'd be."

"Charles?" A voice sounded from the dark house behind him.

"Oh Pearl," cried Molly, opening the door and disappearing into the house.

"Alright, break it down to me. Who did what, why, and where can we find 'em?"

"Naw man. Naw, its Nora. She's..."

"Messin around, huh? See there, that's why we sent Marie on up ta Chicagie. Ain't finsta be taking care nobody's chiren," Charles chuckled to himself, "even if they is my grandchiren."

"Naw man, she ain't messing around. She's gone."

Charles froze, took another pull of his pipe, let it rest on the windowsill and folded his arms. The men stood there a moment. Silent, each in his own thoughts.

"You know 'bout who it is?"

Gideon considered Charles' eyes and they each understood the full extent of the question. Charles had been there those years back. He was there when Lizzy went missing, when they found her body and the determined look of rage on his friend's face. Elizabeth was like a sister to Charles and he felt similar the pain from knowing they'd never see her again. Yes, he was there. He was also there when they drove two dead bodies to the next town and buried them. Everyone assumed Gideon had something to do with the death of his sister's murderers, but no one knew for sure. No one except Charles.

"I'll take care of it, you know that I will," said Charles, speaking in code.

Gideon tucked the pistol into his pants.

"I mean, I don't even know if somebody took her or she done it on her own."

"Well then, we besta find out," Charles picked his pipe back up from the windowsill. "Pearl. I say Pearl!"

"What?"

The two women sat at the dimly lit kitchen table inside the house drinking coffee, and the creases in Pearls chubby forehead buried deeper into her brow at the sound of her name, her lips turned up. Molly suppressed a smile.

"Girl, why you talk to him like that?" she whispered in her friend's ear.

Pearl's face softened. She was a light-skinned woman with full cheeks and a beautiful smile. She rolled her eyes, "Cause he so country. Why he gotta yell my name out there like that for? It's ten o'clock at night."

Molly laughed, "That's yo man though."

Pearl cut her eyes, "Girl."

The women stood and Molly linked arms with her friend, "Uh huh, you know you love you some Charles. Ole country bumpkin!" The women laughed their way toward the front door and exited the house.

"Me and ole Dee gonna take a walk on out here yonder ways."

"Alright," said Pearl.

The men turned to begin their trip off the porch and down the road when they stopped.

"Hey Dad, I tried to warn him, but he wouldn't listen to me," Eddy's tiny voice spoke as he rubbed his eyes. Walter hit him in the side with his elbow, *"Shut up!"* he whispered.

"Hey young fellas, ain't it past y'all's bedtime?" said Charles.

"Walter and Edward. There's a fine switch on that tree out yonder. I am going to get it in sixty seconds." said Gideon.

The boys looked at each other and took off running. Molly ran down the stairs.

"Walter! Eddy!" She ran after the boys before stopping to turn back around. "Pearl, girl I gotta go. These kids done lost they minds."

"You better hurry up then," yelled Charles, laughing and watching the boys speed race to the house.

"Molly, girl wait up. I'm coming witchu."

Pearl ran into the house and back out with her shawl and walk-ran on down the road. The men chuckled to themselves. Watching their women try and catch up to the boys was a sight to see.

"Let's gone and see about ole Ray," said Charles.

CHAPTER NINE

"WHY YOU LOOKING AT THEM LIKE THAT?"

Lisa and Nora were sitting on Charlotte's front porch watching the people across the street. The night was cool and the sun was lowering itself into its chamber, hints of orange and yellows decorating the sky, as the young women enjoyed what was left of the day, preparing to wrap up another taxing session with Charlotte.

"I have never seen any Negroes like that before," said Nora.

Lisa smacked her lips, "But I thought yo family was rich and all that?"

Nora looked at Lisa and frowned, "Rich? I said we had land and animals. Never said we were rich."

"Girl please, land and animals is rich, honey. You ain't gotta go to no store or nothing. Shoot."

Nora thought about her mother's words, *"The White's ain't*

worried none about being happy." She disagreed with that and despised her ancestors' achievements in her heart because it made her parents too proud. They were the descendants of The Free Blacks of Israel Hill. Every winter, when the harvest was brought in and the peaches were canned and the blankets her mother sewed in the summer were ready to make their grand debut, they would all sit by the fire and recite the story with sparkles in their eyes.

In the early 1800s, Hercules White was a slave on Richard and Judy Randolph's Plantation. Before Randolph died, he wrote in his will that his wife was to be given the task of freeing his slaves. Between 1810 and 1811, ninety of the Randolph slaves were set free and given 350 acres of land, which was divided between families over the course of time. Hercules was one of the Randolph's most hard-working slaves and, once freed, helped to pioneer Israel Hill, the all black community of free land located along the Appomattox River in Prince Edward County, Virginia.

Hercules White bought and sold real estate in Farmville, and engaged in other sources of income other than farming. Hercules was a professional business man with five horses and yoke of steel equipped to haul logs, bought supplies for building houses, kept his own records, and grew his own food. Hercules and his wife did well for their time and had four sons: Sam, Tony, Hercules Jr., and Richard. The oldest son, Sam White, was twice the age of the other brothers, and Sam and his wife Susan had fifty acres of their own in the east where the Appomattox and Buffalo Floodplains converged. The land led gradually uphill to Hercules Senior's place in the Southwest.

"Speaking of which, tell me something."

57

Nora raised a brow and blew a breath, "Like what?"

"Like about you, your family. Where y'all from and all that?"

"Virginia. My daddy people was slaves, my mama's too, but the White's were special. Had they own land and everything, owned their own businesses. I guess they was what you'd call rich for back in the day, since many colored people were still enslaved at that time. My great, great, great, grandfather—"

"Dang, you know all yo people, huh?"

"You wanna hear the story or not?"

Lisa laughed.

"Anyway, his name was Nathan. He was the son of Sam White. Anyway, Nathan's daughter, Nancy, was sold back into slavery."

"Shut up!"

"Yup. Even though they were free, Negroes had to be careful in certain areas, where slave patrols were on the prowl for runaways or free Negroes they could sell back into slavery. That's what happened to Nancy. So, her daughter Clara, my grandmother, was born into slavery instead of free like her."

"OK, but that's your dad's mom, right?"

"Yea."

"Was he a slave?"

"Nope. Grandma Clara was freed when she was a teenager and since according to the law, children followed the status of their mothers, Dad was born free.

"But how y'all get to Mississippi though?"

"I didn't tell you?"

"No, you didn't tell me. Spit it out."

Nora laughed, "Grandma Clara was sold away from her mama,

Nancy, when she was a little girl to a slave owner in Mississippi."

"Dang," said Lisa.

"But it turned out to be good because her Massa freed her and gave her land. That's how we got ours. Grandma split the land between my dad and uncles, Uncle Donald and Uncle George, when they got older and got families and stuff. I had an Auntie I never got to meet, Aunt Elizabeth or Lizzy as everybody called her."

"What happened to her?"

"She died awhile back." Nora paused. Maybe she was going too far. She better cut the conversation short. "But don't nobody really know how."

Nora thought back to that night at the dinner table. Gideon and Molly White were proud people and lived well compared to the Negroes around them. *"They didn't carry themselves as if they accepted their second-class citizenship, and they certainly didn't behave as if they felt slave-like in any way,"* Molly would say of The White's. That was a year ago, and Nora shook her head at the thought. There was something not right and she could not put her finger on it. First off, Daddy never let on much about Mama's history. All they ever talked about was the Whites. The White's this. The White's that. It was annoying and Nora wanted to be as imperfect as Mama believed the White's were perfect.

The five acres, home grown foods, brick house, self-sufficiency, and what it took to maintain land bored Nora, and the stories her parents told of the economic freedom it brought was lost to her. To their daughter, farming was slave-like and represented nothing but the servitude to which Negroes were so indebted to whites. To Nora, freedom was leaving the dreadful South to explore the world and all it had to offer—and the world—was Harlem.

"So why you up here? Sound like you had it made."

"No, looks like THEY got it made."

Nora was staring at the people across the street. The women in their layers of light pastel chiffon or heavy velvet, racoon coats, beaded and metal mesh handbags, crystal headdresses and hair ornaments, and lavish shawls. Charlotte lived on Spooner Street, the Sugar Hill of Jacobsville. Suits and dresses, silk and leather, high heels and bow ties, Spooner Street was a brightly lit kingdom, a ten-block stretch of regal row houses and one of the hottest spots in town. It was the place to be for those transitioning their way to Harlem and needed somewhere majestic in which to lay their top-of-the-food-chain heads. If W.E.B. Dubois was white and visiting Jacobsville, this is where he'd stay for the night.

Lisa jerked back, "Who? The Negrolites?"

Nora laughed, "What'd you call them?"

"Negrolites! That's what I call 'em. The "well-to-dos." The "higher ups." The "we-don't-know-what-its-like-to-be-Negroes-no-more" niggas.

"Why do you use that word?"

"Oh, come on Nee Nee, let's not start this again. Like I told you and been telling you since you got here, Negro is just a fancy word used by rich white people in polite society who think they better than the poe white folk. Instead of saying 'Nigger' in public, they say Negro so they sleep better at night. It's the same thing, so it don't make me none difference. Ain't you from the South anyway? You should know this."

"Still don't make it right to say."

"Oh my gosh Nora, really?" Lisa rolled her eyes.

"I'm just saying," debated Nora, "that word gets you lynched where I come from."

"Oh, you ain't heard?" said Lisa.

"Heard what?"

"They just hung a nigga in Harlem last week."

"That's not funny."

"Ain't nobody playing witchu. I'm dead serious. Why you acting all surprised anyway? That's how they gets down around here, baby. Dem white folks ain't having it."

Nora was silent, watching the beautiful men and women as Lisa continued to talk. She wondered if it was worth it, coming here and all. Negroes in the South boasted of the North's overwhelming opportunity. The way they put it, it was kingdom here on earth, but things weren't so simple once you got here. Nora sighed. It's been a year and her dreams of being a famous writer had yet to come true. To start, many of Jacobsville's colored neighborhoods—the ones filled with many of the community's newly arrived Southerners—were slums. Twenty-Seventh to Fifty-Third streets were jam packed with tenants and overflowing with garbage.

Most of the apartments were boarded up and the sidewalks were chocked up with wagons and children running around bare feet and without bottoms. The average Negro worker only earned about seven dollars a week, and the tiny four-room apartments rented for twenty a month. Nora and Lisa were fortunate enough to make ends meet working with Charlotte, who, for all her bossing around, paid handsomely. Thus, they split the rent down the middle, though Lisa afforded an apartment in one of the better areas of Jacobsville.

Located on 134th Street and Lionel Avenue stretched a line of apartments closer to Harlem where the Negro middle class resided. Nora didn't know how Lisa could afford the rent before they both started working, but learned early in life the value of not meddling in other people's business. Besides, she was aware of Lisa's late nights at The Den, a gambling and numbers hole-in-the-wall on Second and Third Avenues. In any event, it was far better than the crumbling, overcrowded shacks of mid-town.

In comparison, Spooner Street was the "Harlem" of town and evoked elegance and class. The streets and avenues were paved in smooth concrete, beautiful apartment homes and brownstones. These faired far better than the ones on Lisa's street. These were new-looking with sidewalks that were lined with trees and signs. Gates locked in the apartments that were finished in High Style. Sadly, Nora knew the folks down South envisioned they'd be living right here on Spooner Street, but nothing could be further from the truth. She was a maid, for goodness sakes, and still awaited the big break that would prove her mother wrong about the North. Speaking of home, Nora felt dizzy, images of her mom and dad floating in and out. Lisa noticed.

"You alright? You know I brought some tea with me."

"Yea, I'm alright." Lisa's therapeutic tea was the bomb and helped to relieve Nora's migraines.

"I think I'm just gonna lay down for a minute since Charlotte on her way out anyway."

"Alright, well we better get back in there since Imma be doing yo work I see."

Nora laughed, "I really do appreciate it."

"I need a drink anyway," said Lisa, getting up as the two women walked into the house. Their ten-minute break was over and Charlotte would be coming downstairs soon to leave for the night and to give her evening orders.

Nora rolled her eyes at Lisa's statement. Lisa hung out with the bootleggers and gained access to the forbidden alcohol. She worried about her friend's over-consumption of hooch.

Just as the women got in the kitchen, the doorbell rang and Nora and Lisa exchanged glances.

"Is Charlotte expecting company today?"

"She better not and ain't tell nobody," said Lisa, her hand on her hips.

"I got a woman, she shakes like jelly all over..."

Nora stopped moving. "You have got to be kidding me."

"What?"

"That's her!"

"Her who?" said Lisa.

"Her. That lady from the train the other day. Remember I was telling you about it? What kinda song is that anyway?"

"Well come on, let's be nosy. I wanna meet your friend."

"That ain't even funny. I must be losing my mind for real. My mama done followed me to New York." The women laughed out the room and watched as Charlotte spoke to the man and the woman from the train.

"Well, if it isn't little ole thang," said the woman looking in Lisa and Nora's direction.

"Thank you for eventually bringing me my coffee. Late as

63

usual."

Nora ignored Charlotte; it was only her fourth cup of the day. Or maybe it was the fifth. She watched as the woman and her white sidekick approached them.

"That's right, I saw you rolling your little eyes at me."

Lisa smiled; she liked her already.

"So anyway, Charlotte, I believe you have something for me," said the woman, diverting her attention.

"And who do I have the pleasure of meeting today?" said the white man.

"I'm Nora and this is my friend Lisa."

"That's an interesting name you have," said the woman, turning around.

Nora remained silent. *"Interesting"* was never the same as good. *"Interesting"* was boring. *"Interesting"* was Lukewarm. *"Interesting"* was in-between good and bad. The last thing she wanted to be was *"Interesting"*. The white man took a bow and Lisa and Nora quickly exchanged looks. They had never been bowed to by a white man before. Nora didn't trust him.

"It is my pleasure to meet you. My name is Carl Van Vechten and this is Zora Hurston."

Nora's stomach twisted, no wonder the woman looked so familiar, "Zora *Neale* Hurston?"

"Like I said," spoke Zora, "your name is *very* interesting."

"Listen," said Carl, "I'm hosting a party at my place for Duke before he heads on up to Harlem. Of course, you are both invited. I would love it if you could come."

"That is so funny! Nora and I have absolutely nothing to do

tonight."

Nora cut her eyes at her friend and noticed Zora tuck some cash into her bra.

"Excellent. I guess you'll be our guest," said Carl.

"I guess so," said Lisa, winking at Nora who felt her feet had stuck to the floor. Nora's mouth couldn't find the words and instead signaled its approval by the stupid smile on her face. Nora promised herself she'd never get star struck and here she was, unable to speak. Even her headache subsided. The excitement remained in her cheeks and right down to her feet, paralyzing her entire body. *Could it be? Was it finally happening?*

CHAPTER TEN

MISSIONARY BAPTIST CHURCH

"THERE GOTSTA BE SOMETHING we can do. I mean, they just can't keep taking our chiren like this, these are our chiren."

Richard stood up and pointed his finger toward the door for emphasis. Molly, Gideon, and the boys sat in the front row while a group of core members were scattered about. A tall peanut-butter toned man stood at the podium dressed in a pair of black slacks and a white T-shirt, modest compared to his typical Sunday wear. His hair was cut low and a gold pocket-watch dripped from his pocket and belt buckle. Pastor Kenneth Johnson raised his arms in protest.

"Now just hold on now Richard, we don't know what the circumstances are now."

"Circumstances?"

"Yes, circumstances. We don't know if someone took her or if she ran away, now just calm down now."

Gideon and Molly didn't attend church except as a meeting place for community news. Gideon felt it was his right to have his Fishing Sundays to himself, *"Besides,"* he'd tell Molly, "most of the church folks sinners anyway. If Imma be a sinner in there, may as well be one out here". In addition, the church served as more than a place to go to hear the preacher talk; it was also the designated meeting spot for the Negroes in Springridge to discuss the issues of race, lynching's, and to come up with strategic plans when it came to securing safety for the neighborhood. The church was a disguise, so the nosy white folks in the town over (most of which were related to the Klan) wouldn't get suspicious about any action they needed to take. It came to be whenever there was a church call that folks hearts jumped into their throats, *"Who is it now?"* they'd say in their hearts, dragging their feet to the church doors and bending painfully to sit in on the next batch of bad news.

"Well, I been in this neighborhood sixty some odd years," Irene rubbed her hand as she spoke, the room breaking out in a series of *"Hmm hmms,"* and *"That's rights."*

"And I don't mean to be rude, Pasta Johnson, 'cause you been good to us. I know you talk to God and all that, but I ain't never seen a missing colored child who just *ran away.*"

The room erupted in "Amens" and "That's sho nuff the truths." Molly kept her hand on her chest as Gideon held her close.

"I wished it was that easy," continued Irene.

"And that's what I say, what we sitting 'round here for? Let's gone and try and find the crackers that done it!" Charles had risen from his seat and had his hand on his waist. Everyone knew what for.

"Won't you just calm down now," said Pearl, tugging at her husband's hand.

"Now I'm down for that," said a young man named Leo. He was Gideon's younger cousin. In fact, pretty much everyone in the room was family.

"We need to go, Unc, for real, sitting here in this church wasting all this time," continued Leo.

"Now don't you go disrespecting the Lord's house now, boy!" scolded Ms. Mary from the other end of the church.

"Well why the Lord let her get took then?" said Leo.

"You ain't too old to get whooped up in here now, boy!" Everyone paused at Irene's outburst. She sat back into her seat and brushed lint from her clothes.

"Mind your manners," she continued.

A few of the women muffled laughter. Brother Earl, one of the deacons, sat close to Molly and Gideon.

"Now when's the last time you say you seen her?"

Molly fought back the tears in her throat, "Like... like I say we was having dinner. And I admit I was harsh on her. I was." Molly paused long as Earl rubbed her back.

"It's alright. Take your time," said another male voice in the room.

"And she was talking that mess about going on up to Harlem, now you know I don't allow that."

"I know that's right," interrupted Irene. Everyone turned to look.

"Well?" Irene raised a brow.

"And so..." continued Molly, "Gideon, he get on up from the table. But I wasn't through with her. I gave her some more, I did."

"You better," said Irene. Everyone turned their faces to her again and then back at Molly.

"And she asked..." Molly's voice cracked, "asked if she could leave and I told her to get outta my face." Molly's voice broke and the crying began.

"That's alright, gone let it out now child," said Mary.

"And the boys were in there doing they reading, so I checked on them but I didn't think about her too much, she a big girl you know. She like laying on under that tree out yonder but I didn't check. I should have checked!" Molly cried into Gideon's breast.

"It's alright, Mama. It's alright."

He tried to hold himself together. To be strong for Molly, but he could not help the visions of his sister that plagued his mind. As much as he tried, and as much as he fought, this present moment he could not help but to compare to the horror many in this same room experienced all those years ago. In fact, he remembered sitting right here, in this same church when they discovered that his sister was missing.

C H A P T E R   E L E V E N

May 9, 1897

"SCUSE ME EVERYBODY."

The church doors opened and everyone jumped, and then calmed. It was just Charles.

"Don't mean to interrupt but uh, Dee? I needs to talk to ya."

A twenty-four-year-old Gideon, much slimmer but the same shade of dark, stood from his seat next to Clara and walked to the door as the men stepped outside. Charles removed his hat and finagled around with the rim, his head was low and his voice shaky. Gideon's friend Ray, and younger brothers Donald and George, stood around them in a circle, prepared to hold Gideon down if necessary.

"Just give it to me straight, man," said Gideon. He hated when people tap danced over the issue. If it was bad, he'd rather have it as is and deal with the consequences later. If it was painful, he'd rather have it in one scoop so that he knew what he was working with; he knew how to deal with the situation and how to digest it. But if it was sugarcoated, it made things worse. He'd have to perceive it as one way, adjust his feelings, only to discover it was a different way. His mother called him complicated, but it seemed to work for him just fine.

A tear escaped Charles' eye, and even though his head was down, he could not conceal it.

"We uh...we found her."

"Is she..." Gideon's voice trailed off, his baby sister's face flashing inside his head.

Finally, Charles looked up and the two men hugged and stayed there a long time. The other brothers gathered around, wrapping their arms around the two friends.

"I can do it. If, if you want," said Ray.

Gideon looked at him, "Naw, I have...I have to," he said, turning toward the church doors and opening them. His friends followed closely behind. Upon their entrance, the people gasped, and their hearts fell into their stomachs. Gideon held his head high, streams of tears cascading down his cheeks. Clara looked on her son and shook her head.

"Get on away from me now, Dee," she was already in tears, which made the emotion her son tried so desperately to hold onto, break.

"Get on away from me, Dee." She said, backing away as Gideon got closer.

"I'm sorry, Mama," he said as the wind whistled underneath the door like lips releasing sighs into the air.

Gideon caught mother Clara right before she fell, and they both crumbled onto the floor as family members rose to their feet to crowd around them. Gideon held his mother as she held onto her stomach. Something heavy was there, like a brick that would not cough itself up. As Gideon held her, he could not truly know the pain weighing heavy from deep inside her body, a ripping of flesh, like a thief come to rid her of the very heart inside her chest. Clara moaned, a wealth of emotions taking over her body and causing her physical pain.

"I wanna see her," the voice was faint.

"Mama, I don't think..." began Gideon.

Clara struggled to break herself loose of Gideon until he surrendered his strength. Slowly, weakly, but determined, she stood and stared her eldest son in the face, "Take me to see my daughter," she commanded.

***

"Dad."

Gideon's thoughts dissipated at Edwards demanding cry. He lifted his son onto his lap.

"Is Nee-Nee coming back?" Walter sat in a seat behind his father, his face in his ear.

Gideon never believed in hiding anything from his sons. If he wasn't real with them, he knew it could mean death. "Hold your head high, but keep your eyes and your thoughts to yourself," he'd say.

"You see a pretty white woman, don't even look at her, keep your eyes to yourself, you understand? And especially, most especially, don't say anything to her. White man disrespects you, let it go. You don't need to be hanging from one of those trees trying to prove how hard you are, understand? Don't matter how old you are; they'll lynch you for good. Lynch, it means to murder without cause and without reason, do you understand? Alright, good. I'll tell you more when you get a lil older. I specs that's good enough for now."

Gideon turned at the sound of Walter's voice, "We hope so, son. We hope so."

CHAPTER TWELVE

"YEA, THEY OUT HERE TODAY, SHO NUFF." Lisa pushed her way through the crowd of people lining the street of Seventh Avenue as the young women shopped around to see what was worth adding to their already full bags. It was Saturday, and they were grateful to finally be off work and enjoying the last part of the day they had left. Residents of Jacobsville headed to Seventh, Eighth and Ninth Avenues to patronize street markets, since Saturday evenings were the only time Negroes had to buy what they needed from the street vendors for their Sunday meals. As usual, the streets were packed. Street vendors operated throughout the week, but Saturday evenings were a busy time as residents shopped on the one day, or part day, they had off from their jobs.

"I don't know what he got in that pot, but it sure smells good," said Nora as they walked over to a pushcart, owned by an older colored man selling soup bowls. There were a surprising number of people out despite the weather.

"It sure does," said Lisa

"Alrighty, what can I do for you?" said the vendor.

"We'll take two bowls," said Nora. "How you like that party though?"

"I dunno. It was aiight, but it seems like that kinda money change people," said Lisa, reaching out for her bowl. Nora watched as Lisa struggled with her bag for enough freedom to cradle the warm bowl the man handed her.

"I thought it was pretty fly," said Nora, dropping the coins into the man's hands and retrieving her bowl. Nora licked her fingers, *colored folk sure can cook.*

Lisa shoved her, "That's 'cause you a writer and all that. I saw the way Carl was parading you around. How yo eyes lit up when he introduced you to all those people. "Whew, this here got some spice to it," she said through a mouthful of soup.

Nora paused and a big smile spread across her face, "Everybody but Langston. Goodness! Where's he hiding?"

"Calm down, girl! Get yo hormones under control."

"I just need to meet him. Like, Z is cool, but she's not the person I'm trying to see right now."

Lisa jerked back, "Who?"

"Z. Zora."

"Oh, so we on a first name basis with Zora Neale Hurston? Dang, ain't know you had it like that."

Nora was silent a moment. She sensed something uneasy in Lisa's statement. She ignored it as the friends continued to shop, finishing their soup and disposing the plastic into the street garbage cans before heading toward Lisa's street as the sun finally disappeared into a heavy slumber, the night sky taking its position as ruler, the moon rising to the occasion.

On Lionel Avenue sat one of the many apartment buildings owned by Phillip Payton Jr., a colored man who took notice of the living situation plaguing the colored community, and thought he'd do something about it. Payton caused friction in small Jacobsville and started a fire when he offered landlords a rental rate above the real estate price. He added a percentage for the rent for himself and was still able to offer apartments at reasonable prices. Payton knew Negroes living in the slums would do anything, and pay anything, to get out of the communities they were in. Once a private area for whites only, 133rd and 134th Streets along Lionel Avenue became predominantly colored as more and more Negroes moved into the flats.

Then there was "Pig Foot Mary," or Lillian Harris who arrived in Jacobsville in the early 1900s. Lillian earned five dollars as a maid. She used three of those dollars and bought a baby carriage and washtub, except Lillian didn't have any babies. Instead, she used the rest of her money to buy pigs feet, secured a position as a vendor along Sixty-First Street, and eventually made a deal with the store owner to cook it for his customers. Pig Foot Mary made so much money that she invested her earnings in property, eventually opened her own Real Estate Company, and purchased apartments just a few blocks from her stand.

Sitting along Black Main Street, where much of the community's institutions were (*Supermarkets, The Negro YMCA, and political clubs*), Lisa's apartment was on the second floor, above a grocery store, to the apartments on 134th Street and Lionel Avenue. The women approached the building, and after speaking to a few of the residents standing around, climbed the stairs to the second floor. The stairway was dark and the way, narrow.

Nora paused, her headache was coming back. *Just make it up the rest of these stairs, girl you got it,* she told herself, ignoring the daze that swept over her hot face. Lisa looked down at Nora and frowned.

"You need to do something about that. Told you Tanya down the street knows a good colored doctor up there on Maine."

"I don't need a doctor. Just a little tired is all."

"What, you pregnant?" Lisa laughed.

"Give it to me!"

The screaming voices of the twins reached the women before they made it up the stairs. The concrete style patios were loitered with old newspapers and candy wrappers left abandoned by tenants who had the privilege to enjoy a full Saturday. There were five or six rooms lining the left and right side of the hall, complete with tenants who couldn't afford to live here alone and often took in roommates to help pay the rent.

A lamp hung in the center of the hallway and Nora rolled her eyes, she hated that it was so dark up here. Tenants did pay, after-all, enough to deserve a little bit of light. The low wattage bulb was supposed to light up the entire floor, but was too dim to do so. The women strutted closer to the voices of the boys and Lisa's apartment, their shoes muffling the sound of being dragged to their deaths by tired feet. Next to each apartment was a food cart. Some of the neighbors had pulled together to get the locals to donate whatever food they had left over to the apartments. Some of the families were extremely poor, spending most of their income on rent and lights just to live on this side of town.

"I said give it back!" yelled one of the boys. They were fighting over a piece of candy. William and Wayne, were ten-year-old identical twins. Nora smiled and Lisa rolled her eyes as they approached the apartment.

"Where y'all mama at?" said Lisa, taking her key out as they stood in front of Apartment 2B.

"She sleep," said Wayne, the youngest by five minutes.

Lisa got the door open, "Exactly. The normal people are in bed and y'all running around here like people ain't gotta get up in the morning." Lisa entered the apartment, and Nora pulled candy from her bag.

"This is yours if you promise me you'll go in there and take care your mom."

"Promise!" said William.

"Wait, you said that too fast," laughed Nora.

"OK, OK for real, we promise."

"Yea, we promise," said Wayne. Nora knew he was just repeating what his brother said and reminded her of Walter and Eddy. She gave them the candy and watched as they entered the apartment across the hall and closed the door.

Nora lingered a moment, and her heart dropped and she felt heavy. In all the time she's lived with Lisa, she never did get to meet the boy's mother. Nora knew the woman was sick, as Lisa had explained, but she wondered who provided child care to the children. Every time she asked them about her, they always said the same thing, "She's sleeping."

"C'mon girl, you letting all my heat out."

Nora stared again, pushing the burning emotion back down her throat before it found its way to her eyes, "Coming."

CHAPTER THIRTEEN

"ALRIGHT, GIRL, HERE'S ANOTHER ONE. THIS HERE FROM CAROLINE DOWN THE ROAD," said Pearl.

Molly rolled her eyes, "Alright, put it on the table."

"Whew, child. You mind if I oblige myself to this here sofa? All this running around, can't be healthy," Pearl heaved in and out as she sat down, lighting a cigarette. She closed her eyes, savoring the nicotine in her throat before releasing it into the air.

Molly chuckled, "Did you just say running can't be healthy?"

Pearl cut her eyes at Molly, smiled, and answered by taking another long pull from the cigarette. Pearl was a big girl, and proud of it. She had a plump backside, wide hips, thick legs, and big breasts. So is the make-up of all the Tate's.

"Girl, you know I can't be losing no weight. Charles will have a fit. Have me walking around here looking all sick like y'all skinny heifers," said Pearl as Molly laughed.

"I'm serious. Shoot, the bigger the berry, the sweeter the juice."

"No you didn't!" laughed Molly. Pearl joined in. She cracked herself up.

Molly glanced over the table, almost completely covered with German Chocolate cake, sweet potato pies, greens, macaroni and cheese, yams, baked beans; you name it, it was here.

"She's not dead, you know," Molly spoke from nowhere.

"What?"

"All of this support. It's like everyone's acting like this is some kinda repass. Like my daughter is dead or something."

Pearl let the cigarette die out in the ashtray. Whatever kinda buzz she had, Molly just blew it.

"They just tryna be supportive is all. You know how country folk are. Your child is their child. The men folk are out looking and the women folk are at home cooking. That's how it is."

"They *will* find her."

Pearl shrugged, "Humph, I know they will. Got the dogs, NAACP and everything else. They better find her."

"I mean alive. They're going to find her alive. I can feel her, Pearl." Molly thought about the last time she saw her very own mother that night on the porch, cold and tired. She wondered for a moment if that's how Nora felt right now: alone, cold, and tired. Molly wanted to feed her. To give her all this food that was made for her.

Pearl sat back on the sofa, *"Here we go again."* She wasn't entirely honest with Molly, but everyone wore the same consensus on their hearts. There was a strong possibility they were not going to find Nora alive. No one wanted to give her credit because she talked too much. Miss Irene talked entirely too much and spoke with an unfiltered tongue, but what she said was true. Children in 1922 Mississippi didn't just run away.

First, no one would let them. Besides their parents, there were just too many eyes watching, which is what makes it hard to believe no one saw anything. This was the South and you had not one parent or two, you had forty, fifty, and sixty. The whole colored community. People looked out for each other and someone, somewhere was always watching.

Still, she didn't know how to break the news to her friend that she should prepare her heart for the unthinkable. Besides, she had her Marie to think about and she didn't know what she'd do if something happened to her. If there was one thing her parents taught her, it was putting yourself in other people's shoes. *"That the onliest way to sympathize wit 'em,"* her father would say. *"You gotta be able to feel where they been, where they walked, and then you can help 'em 'cause you knows. You knows in your heart what they been through and where they is."*

"She gone be alright, Molly. She gone be alright."

Pearl lit her cigarette again, leaned back on the sofa, looked at the table, and prayed her words were true.

CHAPTER FOURTEEN

NORA FLOATED THROUGHOUT THE ROOM. IT WAS SURREAL AND SHE PINCHED HERSELF a few times to make sure it wasn't a dream.

"Whew, not right now. I need a break."

The gentleman walked off as Nora fumbled over to her table, laughing and breathing deeply. She was happy to have worn the the sleeveless metal sequin dress, tan—which blended well with her milk chocolate skin tone—with the nude stockings. The dress had a rounded front and was bare in the back, plunging down to her waist. It was beautiful and easy to move around in. However, the dress was also heavy because of the metal beads. Nora waved her hand in front of her face, catching her breath. She was so happy to have accepted Carl's invitation to the Civic Club. He didn't ask for Lisa which Nora found weird but decided to brush it off. She picked up the glass among the fancy dishes on the table and sipped slowly as the music calmed her bones, washing over her body like euphoria. Nora felt grown-up and sexy.

At New York's only integrated upper-crust club, the book party for Jessie Fauset's first novel, *There is Confusion,* turned into a full-blown celebration of Negro Literature. Charles S. Johnson put it together, and Carl was delighted to invite Nora. He felt this was her golden opportunity, since all the young artists were here: Gwendolyn Bennett, Countee Cullen, Langston Hughes, Alain Locke, Harold Jackman, Zora Neale Hurston (at whose table Nora conveniently positioned herself). They were all here.

Even the old heads came out. In fact, Dr. W.E.B. Du Bois just left the stage. Introduced as the leader of the "Old School", he spoke with a soft seriousness and intelligence. Nora remembered thinking, as he spoke, that his voice matched his face, and she watched the sharp angles of his mustache move against the smoothness of his skin:

"The Negro writers of a few years back were, of necessity, pioneers. And much of their style was forced upon them by the barriers against publication of literature about Negroes of any sort. Tonight, we celebrate the new school from which the time is ripe for organized, determined, and aggressive action on the part of young Negro men and women who believe in Negro freedom and growth."

Next, James Weldon Johnson was introduced as an anthologist of Negro verse, and one who had given invaluable encouragement to the work of this younger group. The real excitement took place, however, when the youngins took to the stage. Cullen's poems received tremendous applause and McKay's, *If We Must Die,* was met with a standing ovation.

Nora's heart stopped when her beautiful Langston took center stage. Zora laughed.

"You know, Hughes is not exactly the lady type."

Nora shot a quick glance at Zora, "What? What does that mean?"

"I mean, you know. Ever seen him with a woman?"

Nora's nostrils flared, "But those are rumors. Langston would never..."

Zora interrupted with laughter and took a sip of her drink. Hughes and Hurston were beefing big over this project they were working on together. Zora said Langston was making a big deal out of nothing. Nora didn't know too much of the details and shrugged Zora's comment off as Langston began to speak. *She probably still has an attitude about it.*

As Langston began *"The Negro Mother"*, Nora smiled. *Goodness, that is a beautiful man.* The entire room was silent, and everyone's breath held still in their throats as Langston continued the rest of the poem. Nora stood and trembled when he finished, clapping her hands with tears running down her cheeks. Everyone else looked at her and followed suit, standing and then clapping, the room erupting in a thunderous noise. The young people were on fire. Langston winked at Nora and walked over to her table.

"That... that was beautiful," she could barely get the words out as the two hugged, and Nora could have sworn she felt his soul, his chest setting flame to her entire body. And she knew then that his heart was genuine.

"Your turn," smiled Langston.

"Whaa, what?"

"People need to see..." Charles Johnson's voice boomed from the microphone, calling everyone's attention back to the stage.

"...people need to see the soul of the Negro to understand him, and that could only be done through the arts."

The room gave applause.

"And the arts could not exist without the continual growth of emerging talent. I would like to welcome to the stage now, a young woman who has flown under the radar, but whose light will shine tonight, as she so wishes..."

Charles smiled in Nora's direction. Her heart stopped.

"Nora White, get on up here."

"I'll go with you," whispered Langston.

There it was, that warmness again creeping over her body, "OK," she said as the two approached the stage.

"I'll be right behind you, on the right side there. You got this."

Nora stared out into the crowd and tried to quiet the thumping sound in her chest that she was sure everyone heard. The blood sped up underneath her skin and the moisture collected under her arms and on the palms of her hands.

"Nora! Kill 'em, girl!" shouted someone from the audience. It was Zora. Always loud, Nora laughed, *"And funny."*

Next, a whistle came, it was from Carl, and Nora smiled and hoped the sweat crawling down her temple didn't make it to the side of her face. She hoped she could remember the words, and that they wouldn't get stuck in her throat. Her heart raced too fast and her feet numbed cold. *I just gotta breathe, I just gotta breathe.* She looked over at Langston, smiling as usual. She imagined no one else was in the room and focused all her attention on that smiling face.

"They get tired of hearing it..."

The room grew quiet, waiting, staring. *Stay focused, they're not even in the room. No one's here. Only him. Sing. Sing poetry to Langston.*

> "Ain't nobody got to say it
> But I knows they get tired.
> Tired of these distractions
> in brown colored skin..."

Someone stirred in the audience, and Nora stole a quick glance at Langston. His eyes were closed. Yes, he was listening. Listening deeply. *Keep singing. Sing to Langston.*

> "Waking up from Valley's
> with muscles and tendons
> all conscious like
> uncovering the blood
> on the American flag
> tired
> tethered
> and intoxicated with
> his
> story
> unraveling the color of bigotry
> on beautiful glass
> smeared fingerprints
> and fallen stars
> like
> why they keep
> sitting in?
> between our comfort

                                        and a hard place
                                                America
                                    this be some kinda
                                                hard place
                            for brown colored skin
                                    in the springtime

Nora didn't remember finishing the poem, for she was floating in and out of herself. *Please not now!* She hoped the headaches wouldn't come and the visions would keep its distance. At one point, she thought she saw her father and wished he could be here to experience this moment. The applause brought her back, forced her to remember that she had finished the poem. Tears spilled from her eyes once more, this time from pure joy as Langston wrapped his arms around her neck, and Zora ran through the aisle. The entire room seemed to jump and the music began to play. It was official, Nora was in. She glanced around the room for Carl, and he winked in her direction. At his wink, the room spun and the dizziness returned.

"Nora? Nora, what's wrong?" Zora slapped the girl's face as her eyeballs rolled to the back of her head.

"Nora!" she shouted, shaking her body.

"Let's get her off the stage," said Langston.

"Come on, hold her head," said Zora.

Nora could hear voices as they clouded her mind. She felt outside of her body. She was floating.

CHAPTER FIFTEEN

WHEN NORA OPENED HER EYES, SHE WAS LAID OUT ON THE MAHOGANY LEATHER SOFA she'd spotted coming into the building. It was in the hallway and off to the side of the main entrance, leaving the walkway clear to walk through. She remembered admiring its beauty coming in. She didn't think she'd have to use it. Zora sat on the other end, her hand holding up her head as she slept.

"What happened?"

Zora raised her head at the voice, "Hey there, sleepy head."

Speaking of head, Nora's was pounding.

"What happened to me?"

Zora sat up, "You fainted."

Nora stood to her feet, wobbling.

"Now hold on now," Zora held onto Nora's arm.

"I need to get back to the table."

"What's wrong now?" Zora, cocked her head back. She did not

come out tonight to babysit.

"I get headaches. The only thing works is Lisa's tea. I got some in my bag." She left out the part that the migrains have been getting worse. Last thing she needed was everyone worrying about her.

"You carry tea around with you?"

Nora sighed, "Please?"

Zora exhaled, "OK whatever, child, c'mon."

The two women held onto each other, taking baby steps back into the ballroom.

"Looks who's up." Nora smiled as Langston walked over to her, "You alright?"

"Yes, and very much embarrassed."

"Oh, don't be," said Langston, "it happens."

"Hey Nora, how you holding up?" said Carl walking over. Nora noticed most of the people were gone, but there was still many lingering around. She locked eyes with Charles from across the room and saw that he was walking over.

Charles walked up, "I can get a driver to take you home."

"Thank you and I'm so sorry for fainting on your stage!"

"Happens all the time," he said winking.

"Will you fools let me get her over to the table?"

Zora was helping to hold Nora up and the girl was getting heavy. Nora giggled as they walked away from the small crowd that started to form.

The rest of the night was exhausting, and yet it was a beautiful kind of fatigue. Nora was officially introduced to everyone; each of them saying how moved they were by her piece and seemed to genuinely care about her well-being. *Told you, Mama.* It was a real dream come true. Nora attached herself to Langston's hip as they mingled with the guest, and was just about to take a well-needed seat before someone else held out their hand.

"So. This is she. I must say, Ms. Nora; I've heard quite a bit about you." Nora couldn't believe she was standing this close to him.

"Dr. Dubois, it is an honor."

"The honor's all mine," said William Edward Burghardt, better known as W.E.B. Dubois, taking Nora's hand and kissing it.

"I must ask, will you come to the Paris Extravaganza?"

"Paris?" Nora looked across the room at Carl; he winked.

"A special presentation on the young and talented of Harlem."

"But I'm not from Harlem."

"What's Jacobsville? Forty minutes away? I think that's close enough."

"Wow, thank you Mr..... Dr. Dubois I—I don't know what to say."

"Say yes," said Langston walking up.

"Hughes," most excellent poem," Dubois held out his hand; Hughes took it.

"My pleasure."

"I do have a question, if I may," interrupted Nora. Carl watched from a distance, inching more and more toward them. Nora's questions made him nervous.

"Of course. Anything."

"What is your concept behind the talented tenth? What are your ambitions?"

Dubois smiled, "My ambitions, well, I like your style Miss Nora! Straight to the point."

"Put it this way, it is impossible to make conclusions merely about Coloreds en masse because not all Negroes look alike you see, think alike or behave alike. And so, the concept is to take the ten percent of the race who have proven highly intelligent, such as yourself—"

Nora smiled as he continued.

"—those who were born free and educated, and do not particularly fit the stereotypical caricature of the southern Negro. And so, the ambition is to organize thoroughly the intelligent and honest Negroes throughout the U.S. to move and guide the least intelligent for the purpose of rights, industrial opportunity, and spiritual freedom."

"Interesting," Nora nodded her head, "but I must say, Dr. Dubois, that it sounds like segregation all over again. I mean, within the races. Separate the ten percent of the intelligent from the what? Ninety percent of the *least* intelligent? What's the reason behind that? How does one determine who's intelligent and who's not?"

"Well, Nora you are quite the guest. Perhaps I can pull you away for a spell?" Carl made his way over to the group. DuBois smiled halfheartedly in his direction before turning to Nora.

"No, quite the opposite. This is not about intelligence. The problem of the twentieth century is the problem of the colored line—the relation of the darker races to the lighter races of men. Surely, we do not wish to create such a separation among the race. The NAACP stands for the rights of men, irrespective of color or race, for the highest ideals of American democracy, and for reasonable but earnest and persistent attempts to gain these rights and realize their ideals. The barrier, however, that we must establish within the race itself is that of the stereotypical Negro. There are some among us who were not afforded certain opportunities, but we must show America that we are not one monolithic group. There are men of such intelligence among the Negro capable of guiding and leading the race as a whole."

"Are you implying that the Southern, 'less educated,' Negro is actually reflective of the stereotypical caricature of white America's view of the Ne—

"I think we'd better have that talk now Nora. I wouldn't want to withhold anymore of Dubois' time. You know, from the other guests."

Nora shot Carl a look, her breathing increasing, her nostrils flared, *Really?*

"Well then, I, for one, am famished," said Langston, using the opportunity to walk away.

"Nora, it was very nice to meet such a powerful young woman like yourself. I wish you well in your endeavors."

"Thank you. It is a pleasure to speak before all of you," said Nora as Carl pulled her away.

"What are you doing?" he said through clenched teeth.

"What do you mean *'What am I doing?'* I can't ask questions, Carl?"

"There's a difference between asking questions and being difficult." Carl sipped his drink.

"Well, the man wasn't making any sense. How do you

encourage a race by separating it? The Talented Tenth? What does that make the other Ninety Percent? *The least talented ninety*?"

"You do know who that is? Whatever opportunity you had, you've just blown it."

"Oh well," Nora folded her arms.

"Nora, you're blowing this way out of proportion and obviously heard nothing the man said."

"Oh no, I heard him just fine. Besides, I happen to be from the South and we aren't any least intelligent than those who were born free."

There was silence as Carl finished his shot. Langston walked back over, nudging Nora in the side.

"Packed yet?" Nora smiled; he was reminding her of the great news. She loved how he just calmed her.

"I was born ready for Paris!" The two laughed as Zora walked up behind them.

"I know that's right!" Nora smiled, remembering the first time she heard that voice. She felt guilty for judging her.

"I, for one, am thoroughly sick of the subject. My interest lies in what makes a man or a woman do such and such and so, regardless of skin color."

Langston put his head down and shook it; he was trying to change the subject. Conversations of race always brought out the fight in people and he did not feel like warring tonight. It was like conversations on religion, never ending.

Nora nodded, "Agreed." She wanted to say more, but there was a respect level she had for the woman in front of her that forced her to leave her opinions lingering somewhere in her throat.

Zora noticed.

"And?"

Nora blushed, "and what?"

"Don't play with me, girl. I have been around long enough to know when a girl's got something on her mind. No sense in being shamed."

Zora held out her arms and led Nora to a table in the middle of the room. Whoever was sitting there was somewhere mingling, and Zora had no care if they returned. As they walked away, Langston called after them, "What, no toast?" Zora waved her hand as Nora smiled.

"Alright!" Zora adjusted her clothing and leaned back in her seat. Her bustling persona made Nora feel happy and giddy. She loved being around people who knew how to have a good time and a good laugh.

"Now we can do some for real talking," Zora pointed to a waiter carrying trays of champagne around the room, "bring that over here!" she shouted as people turned their heads. The man looked indifferent.

"Yes, you. I'm talking to you. The tray, bring it here."

The man complied, lowering the tray as Zora took two glasses, giving one to Nora. The man walked off.

"Now, talk to me," Zora took a sip of her drink, "yeah, this not gonna work. Need some whiskey."

Nora laughed, "You are hilarious."

"And you quiet as hell."

"It's nothing really. I just miss home, you know? I mean it's cool, all of this, but—"

"OK, stop," Zora put her glass down, "don't you do that."

"Do what?"

"Feeling sorry for yourself. If you made a decision, then it's a decision you made. Own it or move on. Ain't no sense being bitter about it."

"I don't think I'm bitter, I just feel real alone out here. It's hard, you know?" Nora took a sip of her champagne.

"Now see that's the problem," said Zora.

"What?" Nora raised a brow.

"I don't think—"

Zora took a sip of her drink and leaned back in her seat.

"—It means you don't know much of anything."

Nora was silent.

"Now I can look back on my life and see highs, lows, and in-betweens. I have been in sorrows kitchen and licked out all the pots, child." The women laughed.

"Then, I have also stood on the peaky mountain wrapped in rainbows, with a harp and a sword in my hands. Point is, lil girl, what I had to swallow in the kitchen has not made me less glad to have lived. To me, bitterness is the odor of weakness, the graceful acknowledgment of defeat. You, Nora, are still young. Whereas, I've been in the kitchen you are there right now, in the struggle with the sword in your hands. If you wanna be here, then be here. If you wanna go home, go home. But don't give off the smell of something dead in the house when you still in there cooking."

Nora smiled, "Meaning?"

"Meaning live, child! Live. You got to get on up now. Get on up and live. You got the sword, don't ya?"

"Yeah, I guess."

"Oh no, see that ain't gonna work. Don't make me embarrass you in here. You know I will."

"Please don't," laughed Nora.

Zora stood up and Nora lowered her face into her hands, "Oh goodness."

"The girl got the sword in her hands y'all!"

Everyone stopped to look at the two women, Langston and Carl laughing.

"Got the sword in her hands and ain't even got the nerve to stand up and fight. Get on up now, child! It's time for you to get up now." Nora's brown skin flashed hints of red and she fell onto the floor with laughter.

"Now y'all see she falling down. We need you to get up, not fall down," Zora fell onto the floor beside Nora and the two women laughed until their sides hurt with painful joy, like girls in their mother's living room. They didn't care that the entire room was watching.

CHAPTER SIXTEEN

"HOLD. I SAY HOLD!" THE DOGS RAN AND BARKED AS THE MEN WALKED, trying to release themselves from the painful grip of the chain. George held on tight, trying not to let his big brothers see the dogs had a hold on him.

"I thinks we should rest awhile," said George.

All the men turned to look in his direction. Pearl was right; it appeared everyone's husband was on the prowl. Some carried their guns on their waist and some their staffs in their hands. Their heavy boots can be heard slapping against the water and slime that caked the wooded area. The trees stood with an ancient strength, tall and thick with long branches; nothing but grassland and twigs scattered at its feet. The dogs barked and sniffed in the wind. Charles ignored George and looked at Gideon.

"What you wanna do?"

Gideon looked up to the sky and the sun told him it was just past noon. There was plenty of daylight left.

"We need to take advantage of all the sun we can. Y'all gone on and rest ya feet, I'll keep looking."

"We ain't stopping if you ain't," said Charles. The men broke into murmurs, "That's right," they said.

"No," said Gideon, "preserve your energy, I'll be alright. Just gonna walk on up."

"You sure?" inquired Donald.

Yes, he's sure! George was still struggling with the Rottweilers, perspiration dripping from his brow. He was tired of the dogs. He was also very hungry. Gideon answered by gripping his staff in his hand and walking forward.

"Alright y'all," said Charles, "let's gone give him a minute."

Gideon pulled down on his hat, shielding his eyes from the sun as he walked onward.

It was a relief to be alone, to have time to think. The news reporter, NAACP, dogs, the whole search was annoying him. He wished only a handful of them were on the search, but Charles had insisted they report it. If only a few of them had come, maybe then things wouldn't be so reminiscent.

CHAPTER SEVENTEEN

MAY 11, 1897

GIDEON HELD ONTO HIS MOTHER, LETTING HIS NATURAL STRENGH AND THE WARMTH FROM HIS CHEST support her frail body. After all, she had been a slave and it was sad to think the cords of bondage still had its hold on her family. A tear escaped his eye, which he wiped away quickly.

The dogs yelped and jerked, forcing Gideon out of his thoughts. George and Donald walked with their heads down, their big country boots stomping into the ground. Ray and Charles walked alongside him and Clara. He was thankful for them and thought briefly about their childhood. They'd all been raised together, and it was as if Clara had borne five boys instead of three.

Gideon looked behind him and smirked; it was funny seeing the Pastor in jeans and a shirt. He was always "suited and booted" as they'd often joke. Kenneth wasn't a pastor to them though; he was just lil ole Kenny, skinny, quiet, and the butt of their jokes.

Charles laughed, "A preacher?"

The boys walked the mile to school alongside the dirt road, looking back every now and again for the school bus. When the yellow peaked around the corner, it was time to abandon the red dirt and jump into the ditch until it passed. If not, they'd all be covered in mud. A game thoroughly enjoyed by the children on the bus, their faces hanging outside the window, their laughter hanging awkwardly in the air while those colored boys wiped mud from their faces.

"What the hell for?" asked Ray.

"A preacher?" asked Gideon.

"Yes, a preacher," said Kenny, scratching his nose.

"Yes, a preacher," mocked Charles, sending laughter into Gideon's chest. *The laughter was worse than the jokes*, he thought, smiling to himself as he remembered.

Ray smacked his lips, "Man, get outta here."

"What's wrong with being a preacher?" said Kenny.

"Nothing if you preaching the truth," said Gideon.

"Man, y'all don't know anything."

"True," said Charles, "but you don't know nothing either."

"I know that Jesus died for our sins," said Kenny. The boys started laughing and Charles fell to the ground.

"Whew. Wait, I can't!" Yelled Charles, between breaths. He was holding his stomach in uncontrollable laughter. Kenny frowned.

"Man, don't you know Jesus ain't his name?" said Gideon.

"Then what is it then?"

"My mama say back then, in the olden days, that the people called him Yahoshua."

"Yahushoowa? What's that?" asked Ray.

"Not Yahushoowa, Yahoshua. HE is the real Messiah. Mama says that's what they called him back then. His name means Salvation. Salvation of Yah," said Gideon.

Charles got up from the ground, brushing off his clothes and looking behind him. There was no sign of the bus, "Who is Yah?"

"Man, don't y'all know anything? Yah is the Father. The Almighty, the Creator."

"Man, shoot. God got many names," said Charles.

"Says who?" said Gideon.

"Says everybody."

"But does the bible say it?"

"I agree with Charles, lot of people say it," said Ray.

"We not talking about people, we talking about the bible."

"There is only one name under the heavens by which we must be saved," quoted Kenny.

"What scripture is that? You don't even know," laughed Ray.

"Acts chapter four, verse twelve," Kenny quoted proudly.

"Ohhhh!" instigated Charles.

"That's my point," said Gideon, "if the bible say one name, how can there be many?"

"What?" Ray was annoyed.

"Does the bible say God has many names or does man say it?"

"What, you a preacher now too?" asked Ray.

"Bible say a lot of thangs ain't true," said Charles.

"It does not," said Kenny.

"You may not wanna say anything else," laughed Charles. Kenny frowned.

"It ain't the bible that's not true, it's the men who teach it," said Gideon, "The Messiah said he has revealed the Father's name to those he gave him out of the world. What name was he talking about?"

"John chapter seventeen, verse two," said Kenny proudly again.

"Verse six," corrected Gideon.

"Alright now, dang. Can we talk about something else now? Kenny got y'all all religified," Charles laughed at his own joke.

"It's not about religion, it's about the truth. If Kenny here's gonna be a preacher, he better makes sure he preaching the truth."

"What about Besse Mae though? I saw her checking you out, Kenny, man," said Ray.

"Yeah, let's change the subject. Kenny, you get you some yet, man?" said Charles.

The boys laughed hysterically. Kenny didn't think it was that funny.

***

Young Gideon laughed at the memories as they walked. Clara looked up, but said nothing. Reminded of the situation, Gideon focused, noticing for the first time that everyone else had stopped walking. Gideon and Clara turned around.

"C'mon, y'all," said Gideon. One of the dogs had his nose in the dirt, and Kenneth followed him.

"Mama, wait," said Gideon, but it was too late. Clara had already begun walking toward Kenneth. Donald ran toward her.

"Mama, Mama wait!" His voice was shaky, and it is at that moment that Gideon ran.

He ran toward his mother, who was running toward Kenny, who ran toward the dog. Everything happened within seconds. The dogs yelped hysterically, some of the men had fallen to their knees, and Clara's screams came out silent. Gideon didn't remember hearing sounds, his feet moving, or the moment he reached his mother's body when it fell. Time slowed down, and for a moment seemed to have stopped. His eyes blurred by tears; it took Ray and George to break him from the trance. There she was, lying lifelessly in Kenneth's arms as he rocked her back and forth. Gideon looked at his mother and the sound came back to him. Charles and Donald had her while George and Ray had their hands on his shoulders.

He scanned her, starting with her feet. She was what they called a "girly girl", so it was no wonder why her toes were well trimmed (and except for the dirt) appeared for a moment—normal. Gideon lingered longer than usual on her feet, afraid to go on. With his mother's screams still in his ear, his eyes went up her leg and washed quickly over her body, and he felt sick.

Her dress had been completely ripped in half, exposing the entire middle section of her body, from her genitalia to her breast. Quickly, one of the brothers handed Gideon his jacket and trembling, he covered her. What he saw next is an image he would spend the rest of his life getting out of his head. There was a brick lodged on the side of Elizabeth's face, pushing her eyes, nose and mouth over to the other side of her face. If not for her feet, and her dress, which Clara made by hand, Gideon's eighteen-year-old sister was disfigured and unrecognizable.

Gideon saw black and was told that he'd fainted.

He didn't cry anymore that day and for days afterward.

CHAPTER EIGHTEEN

"GUESS I'LL FIND ME SOMETHING TO DO SO THE NEGROLITES CAN TALK," Lisa's voice boasted of alcohol as she laughed. Nora sighed. *The Savoy* was packed to capacity as usual, and Nora secretly wished she'd stayed home this Friday night. Also known as "The Home of Happy Feet" and the first racially integrated club, *The Savoy Ballroom* was the most popular dance club in Harlem and stayed packed. While Nora enjoyed the parties, the drinking, and the staying out all night, it was starting to get boring. She was having a great time but she yearned for more literary action. Carl was always throwing parties, and she was always invited, but he seemed to keep her closed off from the good parts. The energy tonight was high and she felt it hard to concentrate. What she didn't need was another one of Lisa's snide remarks.

"You have to do this now?"

Lisa ignored her friend and got up from the table, took another swig of whiskey, puffed on a cigar, and floated onto the dance floor. Nora shook her head. Ever since she landed a small column in *Vanity Fair*, Lisa had been different. If only she knew it wasn't all that. Nora's articles were barely published. When they were, you needed a magnifying glass to see it. At first, she thought Lisa's attitude was the move. Nora moved to Spooner Street to be closer to Carl, where the extra cash from the magazine allotted her an apartment in the row houses. Soon, every time writing was mentioned, she saw the flames of jealousy gloss over Lisa's eyes and she became a different person. She recalled their argument over the Civic Club, and Nora felt bad for not inviting her friend.

"It was just business," Nora had said, leaving out the part where she got sick.

"Business?" Lisa rolled her eyes.

Since then they had not much conversation between them, though Nora was sure to invite Lisa to all the parties since then. Besides, Nora felt a pang of guilt. After meeting people she'd only read about, and being part of Carl's inner circle, the stars didn't light up the sky the way they did in her dreams. She only wrote sparingly in *Vanity Fair* and there were secrets, fights, and restrictions Nora was sure never made the papers. But it was different for Lisa, who was still on the outside looking in. To her the glamour and the glitter still shone like the illumination of the moon against the pitch-black sky. While Lisa knew names and faces, she was not let in on the level to which Nora was now privy and was only tolerated to tag along because Nora had convinced Carl to allow it. And while Lisa was jealous of Nora, there were days Nora herself wished she was still on the outside. Maybe then she could enjoy herself just the same. As she watched Lisa shake it up with a man on the dance floor, she fought the inclination to tell her friend that Harlem was not all it was cracked up to be.

Nora forgot about Lisa a moment and allowed herself to tune into the music. Ella Fitzgerald and Chick Webb were doing their thing with the St. Louis Blues, and the music hung over the room like a cloud and mixed with the whiskey and cigar smoke surrounding the table. Langston sat just across from her and was grinning as usual, and Nora couldn't help but crack a smirk. They became close, best friends, real tight, but not how Nora had hoped. He was close to Carl in a way that confused her and she couldn't understand it.

"I mean, Zora's performance is not very pretty, but I am not surprised. I don't know what you can do. Even if she has entirely re-written the play in a version of her own, she had no right to do so without your permission," said Carl.

"Last night I talked to Zora by phone," said Langston, "she said she knew nothing about French managing the play or how it got to Cleveland. I told her how it got there, and that it came in a terribly different version of the initial writing."

"Perhaps you should put yourself on record as telling a few people what you have just told me."

How about you tell Zora? Nora was sick of their gossiping about her friend, but out of respect for Langston, kept silent. She wasn't sure concerning the trouble with this play of theirs, but she made a mental note to ask Zora about it. Besides, she couldn't lose her cool in front of all these people. Also at the table was Carl's wife Fania Marinoff, Arna Bontemps, Muriel Draper, Jessie Faucet (*unfortunately*), Jean Toomer, and Walter White.

"Since we're discussing works I'm going to be frank with you; I don't like *Good Morning, Revolution*. There are a couple of swell blues and a couple of poems called *Tired*, and *A House in Toas*, (both of which have appeared before and are familiar to your readers). But the revolutionary poems seem very weak to me," said Carl.

What? Nora was confused. She thought *Good Morning Revolution* was excellent. Particularly how Langston personified revolution: *"He knows you are my friend."* Brilliant. Still, she held her tongue.

"I agree. It seems you are venting a bit," said Toomer.

Nora rolled her eyes. Toomer was an interesting person. He preferred neither to be classified as White or Negro, but insisted he was only American. A mulatto by worldly standards, Nora supposed he did have *somewhat* of a point, considering he was mixed with everything. What bothered her was that being American only meant you lived on the continent of America, it wasn't really an identity. Secondly, Toomer seemed to Nora to (while denying the concept of race) move away from the colored classification as much as possible, as if he was ashamed to be colored or something. Unlike Walter who, also biracial, embraced fully his Negro heritage and was working to investigate lynching's in the south. *Go Walter!*

"I disagree with you," Langston addressed the table, "poetry is deeper than tune, but should also embody a message. Many of the poems are not as lyrical as they perhaps should be, but I like some of them as well as anything I've ever written."

"Yes," continued Carl, "but why attack the Waldorf? The hotel employs more people than it serves and is one of the cheapest places to go for someone who wants to go to a hotel."

The Waldorf Astoria was that fancy white hotel in Midtown Manhattan. Nora remembered the Negroes in Jacobsville complaining about their policies. She took a sip of her wine as she watched the men go back and forth.

Langston laughed, "I believe that you told me that the dining room was so crowded that first week that people could barely get in and that the bread lines were so long that people couldn't reach the soup kitchens for a bowl of free and watery soup."

"Well, doubtless I'm wrong, but this is the way I feel about things. You asked me to read the poems and give my opinion, and there it is. I have no quarrel with you linking the American Negro to communism if you want to."

"Well, I am willing to revise the book, omitting some poems and putting in a few new ones."

"What?" Nora couldn't take it anymore, "I think the poems are very well written, particularly, *Good Morning Revolution*."

"Thank you, Nora," Langston winked and Nora melted.

"I think it's possible to be a good revolutionist and a good poet too, but the present book seems calculated to appeal only to those who are already in agreement with it."

Did he just...? Nora burned a hole in the side of Carl's face as he took a sip of his liquor, ignoring her stare as silence befell the table, leaving room for the music to finally have its place. Since they were all here, Nora thought this was as good a time as any to bring up something worth discussing. Besides, Carl's voice was getting on her nerves.

"You need to change the name."

"There it is," chuckled Langston.

"I'm serious. Carl, you need to change the name."

"As we've advised repeatedly," said Walter.

"I don't see what all the fuss is about," said Fania, "it's his book."

"Nigger Heaven, Carl?" Nora ignored his wife. If she had any sense she'd be more worried about her husband's sexuality, which was questionable.

"Does anyone care to be informed on what the book is actually about?" said Carl.

"We know what the book is about: Niggers."

Jessie spilled her drink and burst into laughter.

"If you write as raw as you speak, *The Crisis* will have a time indeed."

Nora turned up her lip, "I have no interest in *The Crisis*."

Nora's own words were a shock to her own ears. As much as she sat by that window at home and re-read page after page of Dubois' paper, her encounter with the man and experience in the movement left her unimpressed. Besides, Jessie got on her nerves. She had been working as the literary editor for the magazine since 1919, but Nora thought she had a stuck-up attitude.

"Oh? Good Carl, it sounds like you won't have to pay the rent this month. Nora's got it all under control."

"Excuse me?" Nora stood up, ready to show Ms. *Thang* what colored girls from Mississippi could do to her face. She didn't mind being immature when it came to defending herself. She was, after all, an eighteen-year-old pretending to be twenty-five. It was Carl's idea, and with his connections—he and Langston knew pretty much everyone between them— it wasn't difficult to secure the paperwork.

"Nora, c'mon, let's get some air," said Carl.

Jessie winked and raised her glass as Carl pulled Nora away from the table, and they walked toward the door.

Lisa saw Nora leaving with Carl and raised a brow.

Oh, so that's what we on?

The man she was dancing with grabbed her arm, "Hey, baby, you alright?"

Lisa looked at him like he was a stranger, ignored his question, and stormed away.

Nora and Carl stepped outside the club to a full street, and the cool air wrapped around their bodies. The streets were its usual hustle and bustle—jam packed with cars, men, and women both Negro and white standing around with their fancy clothing and jewels. The men stood in their suits made of several different materials, from linen and wool to leather, defined shoulders and narrow hips, bows, and ties. The women too, with their rhinestone decorated dresses, silk gloves, and high heels.

The clubs lit up with bright white lights and the music echoed from inside out. If for some reason you weren't allowed inside, that was alright. It was exciting just being on the street, for it was a party in and of itself. Just as Carl and Nora began to speak, Lisa brushed past them.

"Lisa!" yelled Nora, and Lisa spun around.

"That's what I am to you now? You just gonna leave me here?" Nora looked at Carl with a frown; it had to be the liquor talking,

"What are you talking about? I'm not going anywhere."

"Wake up Nora!" shouted Lisa as she walked alongside a gentleman who led her to his car.

"I can't do this anymore."

"She'll be alright."

"I'm not talking about Lisa, Carl. I can't do this anymore. This life."

"These kinds of things take patience, Nora. Success is not just going to fall into your hands. Just wait; they'll see what you can do."

"I'm not talking about that. Are you going to change the name, Carl?"

"No, I'm not going to change it. It's not what you think. Goodness Nora, Nigger Heaven; it's what Harlem is."

"Listen to yourself!" Nora folded her arms, tapping her foot against the concrete. There was a brief silence.

"We sit in our places in the gallery of the New York Theater and watch the white world sitting down below in the good seats."

"We? Are *you* in the gallery, Carl?"

Carl paused, ignoring Nora's tone, watching as the world went about its business. He couldn't lose Nora. Her work complimented Langston's so well. He took advantage of the silence and continued.

"And it never seems to occur to them that Nigger Heaven is crowded, that there isn't another seat, that something has to be done."

"I get it," said Nora. Carl looked at her, surprised but relieved.

"No, seriously, I do. Harlem is Nigger Heaven. Nigger's wanna go to heaven, so they come to Harlem where they can sit up on the top, in the balcony," Nora looked around her, "but away from the music. In the balcony. Close. Just not close enough."

"What?" Carl hoped she was coming to her senses, but now she wasn't making any sense.

Nora thought a moment. Nigger Heaven. She finally understood what Dubois meant by The Talented Tenth. The ten percent were those Negroes of higher education and higher status. They were the doctors, lawyers, and professional men and women of the race, and they stood as guards above to protect the ninety percent of the low class beneath them. They were the business men and women of Harlem, the gate keepers. Except, there was nothing privileged about colored folk having to watch the movie from the balcony. It only separated them from being able to see what is close to the ground. The ground. That is where many of the colored folk were. Poor, destitute, and living in slums. It is impossible for the upper class of her race to relate to these Negroes being so far up, away from their struggles. No, one cannot help being so far off the ground like that. One can only look down upon.

CHAPTER NINETEEN

"YOU ALRIGHT, MAN?" GIDEON JUMPED AT THE SOUND OF CHARLES' VOICE, streams of tears falling from his eyes. He'd been so caught up in the past that he hadn't seen Charles walk up. He'd walked about a half a mile from the group and stood now at the lake. It was a beautiful place to sit, think, and on occasion, fish.

"You 'bout ready?"

Gideon turned to face him and seeing his tears, the two friends hugged for a long time, crying on each other's shoulder.

"It's about time. It's about time," said Charles. Gideon had held on to Lizzy long enough. It's about time he cried for her. Gideon looked at the sun; it didn't shine as bright as it did before.

"How long was I gone for?"

"Oh, we been resting a good half hour. The men needed it though. Ole Kenny and Mike brought back some food. Thinks we best get back to it now."

Gideon smirked, "Brought back food? With all the cooking dem women folk doing?" The men laughed. They both knew it didn't matter to Brother Mike. He always had food hid away somewhere and he was always ready to eat. Gideon's stomach growled, "Yeah, let's head on back."

The men turned away from the lake and headed back toward the group. Gideon laughed.

"What's up?"

"Nothing, just thinking. Good thing Molly didn't come with us. This is me and Nora's home away from home. Wouldn't wanna give away the spot!" The men laughed.

"I must say, Dee, I admire y'all's relationship. If Marie just had half the sense as yo Nora."

Charles paused, "Wait, did you say this was y'all's *home away from home?*"

"Yeah, so?" Gideon barely got the words out as Charles took off running back into the direction of the lake.

CHAPTER TWENTY

"WHAT ARE YOU TALKING ABOUT? I WASN'T GOING TO LEAVE YOU. Why would I do that?"

Lisa threw off her wig, "Nora, I really don't care. I mean sure, I've carried you all this time, put food in your belly, money in your pocket and this is the thanks I get? Naw, you good, girl. I'm cool. Go back to your fancy apartment Carl's paying for on Spooner Street." There was a pause. "They don't even like you, Nora."

"I know that. This is why I'm not working for Carl anymore. *Vanity Fair* is over. I'm done."

Lisa moved about the apartment in her thoughts. She was happy, but didn't want her attitude to get in the way of Nora's success.

"I am proud of you. You know that. But these people, I just don't know. And from what you've told me?"

Nora plopped down on the sofa, "I know. I don't know what to do. Thinking about telling Zora about the whole play situation."

"Stay out of it, Nora. This is what I'm talking about. Why can't you just leave it alone?"

"Stay out of it? I'm in it, Lisa. There's just a lot you don't know."

"Oh, I see."

"I don't mean it like that. I'm just saying, I'm in deep."

A silence fell over the room and Nora could sense the jealous tension squeeze itself into the spaces. She wanted so desperately to share with Lisa, but Lisa's mouth was unfiltering. She couldn't risk anything getting out. *Maybe if I just let her in on a little something. She must know things are not what they seem.*

"You know they on Charlotte's payroll."

"Who is on what?" Lisa said as she looked through the mail. She'd had enough of trying to raise somebody else's child. Nora needed to get it together.

"Langston and Zora is on Charlotte's payroll."

"Our Charlotte?" Lisa walked over to the sofa and sat down, a pile of mail still in her hand. Finally, some juicy information.

"You remember that day we met, right? When Carl invited us to his party? And you remember when Charlotte gave Zora the money?"

"Money? What money?"

"Lisa, girl you gotta start paying attention. That day Carl and Zora came over to the house, Zora was tucking away some serious cash."

"OK, so? Get to the point."

"One of the main ways Charlotte makes her money is by funding Negro artists. Zora told me all about it. Sometimes rich white folks invest in a colored person's career when they know they got talent and they call themselves patrons, but Zora calls them Negrotarians."

"Negrolites, see I told you."

Nora laughed, "No, the Negrotarians ain't the Negroes, they the white folks who fund the Negroes."

"Same thing," said Lisa. She was glad they were talking again. Nora continued.

"So anyway, there's some serious tension between Zora and Langston."

"Right, over the play thingy."

"Yea, but that's only half of it. Not only is Charlotte paying Zora more than Langston, but word on the street is that she about to cut him off."

"Gone?" Lisa was shocked.

"Gone. Like, cut off. Carl was saying something about Langston about to move back in with his mama."

"Charlotte got bread like that?"

"That's why she wanted us to call her Godmother. She tells all the Negro artists she funds to call her Godmother."

"OK, but that don't make sense though, we not artists."

"You think Charlotte didn't know I was a writer? Langston pulled me to the side one day and offered me a chance to work with her. She was using him to get to me."

"And you didn't take it?" Lisa scrunched her face.

"I know we were struggling, but I'm not for sale. My mama already told me about these white folks up here. Plus, giving them money is not all she's doing. She controlling they whole thing. She decides what they can publish, what they can't publish, and everything. I've seen some of these writers come by the house begging her for money they earned. I ain't got time for that."

"First of all, some of us still struggling," Lisa said, laughing with sarcasm as she got up from the sofa, the mockery in her voice lingering behind. The negative energy may as well have been sitting in the dent she left in the sofa. Nora ignored it and thought about Carl and Langston's conversation earlier, and shook her head, *Yea, Carl you ain't slick. You one of them Negrotarians too. Why else you all up-Langston butt? Mama ain't raise no fool.*

"Well," said Lisa, "before you do anything too stupid, you got another letter." She tossed the mail on the sofa and walked away.

Nora smiled, "Did you open it?"

"Don't judge me!" yelled Lisa from the back room. Nora laughed as she flipped it over and ripped it open:

Molly White

Nora spread her body across the sofa, holding the letter close to her chest.

"Not yet, Mama. Not yet."

CHAPTER TWENTY-ONE

"HEY, MAN, WAIT UP."

Gideon hurried to catch up to Charles who was digging his way through the water.

"Dee," Charles called to him as his body sunk deeper into the water.

"Dee!"

"I'm coming," said Gideon, wading through the water, his legs feeling like there were weights tied to his ankles. Gideon thought water was an interesting mystery. It could destroy you or save your life.

He made it to Charles whose arms were already immersed into the lake.

"The other side. Grab the other side!" he yelled.

Charles directed Gideon to help him to lift the heavy object out of the water as the waves moved back and forth and the wind blew strong.

"One, two, three!" The men allowed their strength to lift the object up and out of the water, and a large tree limb became visible. The men dropped it.

"I'm sorry, man, I thought," began Charles. He was at a loss for words, an event that rarely happened.

"Naw, it's alright," said Gideon as the men stood in the water, "let's go head on back."

CHAPTER TWENTY-TWO

"WHAT ME AND LANGSTON GOT GOING ON AIN'T GOT NOTHING to do with you." Zora stormed into the apartment and waved papers in his face.

"What's the matter with you?" Puzzled, Carl closed the door.

"Ain't what's the matter with me, it's what's the matter with you. You got no business discussing what me and Langston got going on Carl, no business!"

"Zora, calm down," he sat at the red oak desk with the shiny reddish finish and tried to recall the last time he'd offended Zora. He really tried not to, on account of her temper.

"Langston and I are good friends with a good understanding."

Zora slammed the papers down in front of Carl's desk. They were letters he'd written to Langston. Their discussion was *The Bone of Contention* and their language about Zora was far worse than what was discussed at *The Savoy*. Carl's face turned red and he felt hot.

"How did you get this? Where did you get them?"

"It don't matter how I got 'em. Now for y'all's information, I talked to Langston. Wrote him six typewritten pages and talked to him long distance. AND for y'all's information, I don't think the play need to be did in Cleveland no how. You'd know that if you were talking to me and not him."

"Zora listen," started Carl, but she turned her back.

"I don't need yo explaining, you did enough of that in those letters there, but you tell that lil girl of yours she better watch her back."

Zora stormed out of the door, slamming it shut.

Carl sat at his desk and froze, *Girl of mine?* He searched his thoughts and the truth iced cold on his face.

"Nora."

CHAPTER TWENTY-THREE

"I'M SORRY, BUT THE TRIP IS CANCELED."

Nora wrapped her hands tight around the warm cup. Wells Supper Club was only half full which, aside from Langston's attitude, was unusual. A family-owned establishment, Wells was known for its southern-inspired menu and served as the cornerstone of the Harlem Food scene. Nora had been here plenty of times on late nights with the Jazz musicians, bands, and party goers who partied late into the night. Wells offered breakfast, lunch, and dinner, but profited from its creative blend of a late night/early morning menu for the party goers. Wells featured its southern fried chicken paired with its deliciously sweet waffles. The Chicken and Waffle combination became a hit that many restaurants would mimic.

"Can't say I didn't see that coming," Nora tried to be optimistic in front of Langston, but the news hit her stomach like a rock and weighed her down. She was looking forward to leaving the country.

She was looking forward to Paris.

"You should have."

Nora looked into those gorgeous eyes. Langston never spoke to her like this before.

"What are you talking about?"

"Nora, what you did was wrong. You owe both Carl and myself an apology. I would say you owe Hurston too, but she won't hear of it."

"First Carl drops me from the trip—". Surprise crept into Langston's face.

"—Yes, I know. Walter said you all were still going."

"I didn't find out until last night," said Langston.

"You knew though. So, like I said, Carl drops me from the trip, stops my money flow so I have to move back in with Lisa—"

"Nora, that's not fair. *Vanity Fair was* your money flow. You left, remember?"

"—and now you're asking me to apologize?" continued Nora, ignoring Langston's point.

"Carl is not a perfect man, but you had no business talking to Zora, who, by the way, came by my place waving manuscripts in my face."

"I had no business talking to Zora like you and Carl had no business talking *about* Zora."

"Spare me the dramatics, Nora. Because of you, Zora probably won't ever speak to me again." Langston's voice was calm, but firm. "It's not your job to look out for us, Nora. You're still new to this."

"I see," Nora folded her arms.

"You know what I mean. You think you've got it all figured out but you have no idea what's going on. Zora and I started this project together and now she's going off as if it's hers alone. Listen, Hurston contacted me when we were both doing our traveling and asked me to work on a script with her. We'd heard that Theresa Helburn..."

"Who?"

"Of the Dramatists Guild."

"Oh," Nora still didn't remember. She met so many people and barely recognized their faces, let alone their names.

"Helburn was looking for some uplifting Negro material for a play, and that's when we decided to work on Hurston's material and came up with *The Bone of Contention,* which she is now calling *Mule Bone.* The work was coming along well, and then Hurston out of nowhere disappeared. She left the manuscript unfinished to do some folk research down South. Frustrated, I just left it alone. I was already dealing with Charlotte and her relentless control over my work."

"So, the script *was* Zora's."

"Nora! That's not the point. She submitted work that included Acts written by me. She had no right to submit a play that we worked on as a team as if she did it by herself. We were on the bridge of rectifying this situation until you stepped in. This, Nora, is the kind of thing that happens when proper communication is non-existent."

"Well, I'm sorry I upset you."

Langston stood, pulled his coat from around the back of the chair he was sitting in and draped it on.

"I'm sorry too. You obviously still have much more to learn.

You're brilliant, but young. What am I to do the next time you decide to stick your nose in someone else's affairs? These kinds of mistakes can have very cost-effective results in this business. Goodbye Nora."

Langston Hughes walked out of the restaurant, his coffee only half consumed. Nora watched his driver open the door and tears escaped her eyes as the car sped off. She leaned her head back against the chair, it was pounding and she felt dizzy with nausea. She wondered if she should take Lisa up on her offer to ask Tanya about the doctor. If she had anything to fix now, it was a broken heart.

CHAPTER TWENTY-FOUR

"HEY, DEE, DEE!" DONALD'S VOICE PENETRATED THE AIR AS HE RAN UP TO THE MEN. Clara was sure her son's voice could be heard for miles and miles on end. Maybe from state to state. When he was little, she had to stop him from talking so loud so she wouldn't think anything was wrong.

"Dee." Donald was out of breath, his hands on his knees as he bent over, chest heaving in and out.

"What's up?"

"I think they found her."

Gideon exchanged looks with Charles, "Where?"

"Somebody say they saw someone fitting her description over there by the King building."

"The hotel?" said Charles.

"Downtown?" said Gideon.

"Yea, the King Edward Hotel downtown. A colored man said he

seen her. Some elevator operator for the hotel, think they say his name is Frank something."

"Imma go get Molly," said Gideon, running.

Charles watched his friend run on and could only imagine the kinds of thoughts that must be running through his head, *not this again.*

CHAPTER TWENTY-FIVE

"DON'T WORRY ABOUT IT. I'M GLAD YOU TOLD ME," said Zora, staring down at a red-eyed Nora, sitting chicken-wing style on her floor with her legs crossed.

"How did you get the letters anyway?"

"When Carl invited me to the Civic Club," Nora stopped to remember, wondering if he still had those ugly venetian seats in the dining room. She shook her head, "I pretended to go to the bathroom. What I really did was sneak into his office." There was silence a moment. "I'm sorry," Nora wiped at her eyes.

"And stop apologizing."

"I just feel so stupid. I messed everything up."

Zora looked at the young woman in front of her.

"Personally, I know what it's like. I'm sure I could be a better friend in certain situations myself. I keep seeing new heights and depths of possibilities which ought to be reached, only to be frustrated by the press of life which is no friend to grace."

Nora cradled her face in her hands and smiled. She loved when Zora spoke this way. There was so much experience sitting across from her, and she intended to soak up as much wisdom as the woman would allow. As Zora spoke, Nora wondered if she'd missed her blessing. Here she was, sitting in the living room of one of the leading artists of the Harlem Renaissance. Even though things were not shaping up as she thought they would, as far as her own dreams were concerned, Nora was living history and wanted nothing more than to cling to Hurston. If she could hold hands with her and lay her head on her shoulders while she told Folk stories, she would do so for a lifetime if she could get away with it, like a child clings to its mother's breasts. In Zora's absence, Nora's heart ached to hear her speak and for her to prophesy into her life.

"I have my loyalties," continued Zora, "and my selfish acts too, and I ain't never been perfect or nothing lak that. But I have also received baffling friendship that is satisfying. So many people have stretched out their hands and helped me along my way."

Nora dropped her hands, "I knew there was something about that Carl. I never trusted him."

Zora looked directly at Nora, "You watch that mouth of yours. With the exception of Godmother, Carl Van Vechten has brawled me out more times than anyone else I know. He's not one of those 'white friends of the Negro' who would earn his place by being all up in our face. Exceptionally complimentary and the like. If he is truly your friend, he will point out your failings as well as your good points in the most direct manner."

"Like that time at the club?"

"You shouldn't go telling folk's business like you do, but yes, like that time at *The Savoy*. Langston's no newbie to the likes of Carl. The two exchange opinions of the sort all the time. Langston wants to know if his work is good and Carl gives it to him straight. No chaser. Take it or leave it. If you can't stand him that way, you need not bother. It is the best of friends who get into fusses of the like all the time. You and that Lisa of yours can't stop arguing now can ya?"

Nora laughed before her face got serious again, "But there is something I don't get, why does Charlotte pay you more than Langston and why do you insist on calling her Godmother? That just seems so racist to me."

"Remember when I said you needed to stay outta folk's business? You'll have all kinds of drama following you in this business, and stress too, if you concerned yourself with why this person is doing such and such."

There was a pause as Nora's cheeks turned red.

"But to answer your question," continued Zora, "yes, sometimes, I feel discriminated against, but I don't let it take away from my peace. It merely astonishes me. How can any one not like me? It's beyond me."

Zora laughed and Nora cracked a smile too. When the women composed themselves, Zora continued.

"But, like I told you, don't depend too much on skin color. You'll certainly get distracted if you depend too much on that. I've been betrayed less by whites and more by those who look like you and me."

"All my skinfolk ain't kinfolk," continued Zora, laughing.

Nora laughed too, but then her smile faded away. She looked at Zora laughing and felt a closeness to her that she didn't for her own mother. Her stomach churned and she felt guilty. Here she was secretly wanting Zora to be more than just a friend when she had her own mother. Was it selfish to want two? Could she pretend as if she's come from another womb without betraying another? Where was the line? Nora's throat felt dry and the tears rose to the occasion. There wasn't anything special about the first time she saw her. But then, there was. She missed Molly White.

CHAPTER TWENTY-SIX

AUGUST 19, 1922

THE THUNDER GROWLED AS MOLLY SHUT THE CAR DOOR AND RAN INTO THE HOUSE with the platter in hand.

"I'm sorry, baby," she said, almost tripping over someone's foot as she made her way to the kitchen table.

The White home was packed for what seemed the fifteenth time to Molly this week. Men violated her shiny floors with their hammer-like feet; women suffocated the air with their gossip; Kenny sucked what little joy from the room with his preaching to everyone who would listen; Walter and Eddy ran back and forth with their friends as if her house was an amusement park and the front door a slide; Pearl laughed at her own jokes; and everyone just spoke far too loud. News of Nora's whereabouts sent waves of response throughout the neighborhood, and they were all here to get the scoop on what happened. The hairs stood up on Molly's neck and arms.

Not everyone was here out of sympathy and concern. In fact, she knew that half the room was here as transporters of gossip. They wanted to know if it was true what they say about the Whites, and Molly was on edge. She'd tried separating herself from that part of her family history as much as possible. That is why she always talked about the good parts. It never occurred to Molly White that people craved a little drama. They thirsted for it, needed it like air and would go so far as to create it, if need be. As much as Molly spoke good and tried to keep a happy smile on her face, nothing was always as good as it seemed. Not even the prestigious Whites.

Molly sat the dish down on her full table and stared out in space; dark lines spread out underneath her eyes.

"Now Ms. White, why don't you gone and get you some rest now?"

"I appreciate that Miss. Irene, but you know I can't do that."

"Well, can't say I didn't try," smiled Irene, patting Molly on the back.

"Alright girl, Gideon's back," said Pearl, walking up as Irene walked off, "you need help with anything over here?"

"Nope, I think everyone is pretty much taken care of."

"You sure about that?"

Molly scanned the room, "Yeah, it's alright in here today."

Pearl touched Molly's arm, "I mean you. Are you alright?"

"Molly?" Gideon's voice interrupted from across the room and Molly smiled, "We'll talk later."

"I'll be here."

Molly walked over to Gideon and as the couple embraced, she inhaled deeply, wanting to consume the strength emanating from the heat of his body.

"We think they found her," he whispered.

"I know. Is she..."

"Alright, everybody listen up," Gideon left Molly's question to hang around with the rest of the tension in the room. People from every corner of the house stopped to give Gideon their attention.

"Wait, where's that knuckle head Charles at?"

Pearl giggled, "You know I can't keep up with that ole fool." Gideon smirked and shook his head.

"Alright, everybody settle down now. We have word that someone fitting Nora's description has been spotted downtown."

The room erupted in praises and applause. Gideon held up his hand, "I'm not finished."

The room quieted.

"We don't know if the person is actually Nora yet, but this person has been found alive."

The house erupted into joyous applause again and Molly fell into Gideon's arms.

CHAPTER TWENTY-SEVEN

MOLLY WAS STILL KISSING HER HUSBAND WHEN SOMEONE KNOCKED ON THE DOOR. She rolled her eyes, "Where is all these people coming from?"

Gideon smirked, he loved his wife's realness, "I'll get it."

Molly shook her head, but she was not as annoyed as she would have been had the knock came ten minutes ago, her heart still rejoiced at the good news. Nora was safe and that is all that mattered.

"Anybody know a Gideon White?"

The house turned its attention to the voice with the deep southern drawl coming from The White's front door. It was all too familiar and Nora moved closer, standing behind her husband. Two Sheriffs stared back at them, one of them spitting brown tobacco on the ground. Gideon's blood raced and his jaw locked.

"I'm Gideon, who wants to know?"

The tobacco chewing officer pulled handcuffs from his back pocket and reached for one of Gideon's arms. Dee jerked away.

"Don't make this any harder on yourself there *White*," mocked the officer. The room erupted into gasps as people placed their hands over their mouths.

"What?" Gideon stepped back into the house.

"What? Why?" Molly held onto Gideon's arm.

The officer responded by snatching Gideon's arms and twisting them behind his back, slapping on the handcuffs.

"No," said Molly shaking her head.

Gideon looked at his worried wife, "It's alright," he whispered.

"No, no it's not." Molly's voice was shaking as she directed her attention to the officers, "What for!" She didn't realize that she was yelling as she held onto Gideon's shirt. She also didn't hear Pearl walk up.

"What's going on here?"

The sheriffs turned Gideon around, yanking him out of Molly's grip.

"Get Charles," he whispered, before they yanked again and started down the steps and off the porch of the house.

"What's going on is this man's wanted for murder," said the other officer, wearing a sinister smile as they approached the vehicle.

"What!" Molly screamed the words as everyone began to file out of the house and spill into the street. The entire neighborhood stood on their front porches and in their front lawns. Some of them shook their heads and swept their porches in silent celebration. Their facial expressions and folded arms screamed *"I told you so's"* and *"I knew that nigga wasn't no good"* and *"That's what they get for being so uppity."*

"Mom, where are they taking Dad?" said Walter with Eddy following behind.

"C'mon babies, your dad said to get you on into the house now," said a neighbor, ushering the children back into the house. Walter frowned his face, he didn't hear Dad say such a thing.

"No, please. Please!" yelled Molly as Pearl and Miss Irene held onto her arms.

"C'mon now, Miss Margaret, everybody's watching. Don't give 'em nothing to talk about," said Irene, tugging onto Molly's shirt.

"Damn them!" Molly yelled out into the streets and into the conscious of those whose eyes had held the stones of their condemnation of her family for so long. "Damn all of you!" she screamed out through blinding tears.

"Whole damn family's crazy," said the officer, stuffing Gideon's large body into the back of the vehicle, "let's get this nigger out of here."

The car drove off down the road and Pearl let go of Molly to meet a running Charles halfway.

"What's going on?"

"I don't know. They took Dee, I don't know," said Pearl, fighting back her own tears.

"Calm down now and tell me what happened."

They reached the house just in time for Charles to lock eyes with an older man in the distance. No one noticed him standing off to the side.

"The hell?"

Molly cried into Charles' chest as they approached the front porch, and the people didn't move for a chance to miss out on what would be the talk of this year. No one noticed as Frank walked up and brushed past Charles, whispering something that made his eyes buck as he zoomed past him.

Charles turned only to see the back of the old man's jacket. He didn't even catch the back of his head as the rain started pouring down.

CHAPTER TWENTY-EIGHT

LISA'S APARTMENT

THE SUNLIGHT BLINDED NORA AS IT SLICED THE DARK ROOM, a silhouette of Lisa standing over by the window, pulling back the dull beige curtains she hated so much and revealing more of the wide, open windows.

"Girl, why you sitting here in the dark? And why you not up yet?" The sun spilled through the windows, illuminating the apartment with splashes of light. Nora closed and then rubbed her eyes.

"My head is killing me." She sat up on the sofa and took a sip of Lisa's tea, she felt sick.

"That's it. I'm going to get Tanya."

Nora stood and she could hear the voices of William and Wayne in the hallway.

"Alright already, settle down." Nora grimaced; their voices pierced her ears and went straight to her head, cracking it just a little bit more.

Lisa looked on, her lip twisted up, "Who are you talking to?" Nora held onto the sofa. "The twins. All they do is argue. It's killing my head."

Lisa looked at her friend like she was a small child.

"Umm, Nora?"

Nora took a deep breath and held onto the sofa. She was making up her mind on whether she should walk to the kitchen.

"What?" Lisa's voice was annoying her. She wished everyone would just be quiet. Where'd all these voices come from?

"Nora, the twins are not here. Do you know where you are?"

Nora rolled her eyes, what kind of question was that? Of course, she knew where she was. She smirked, "And you say *I* need Tanya." Nora took a couple of steps toward the kitchen and collapsed onto the floor.

"Nora!" yelled Lisa.

CHAPTER TWENTY-NINE

"SUSIE LOCKLEAR WAS A SLAVE," SAID MOLLY.

The rain forced everyone to go back to their corners of the world, closing their doors and whispering among themselves about The White's misfortune until next year's event.

"Molly, don't," began Pearl.

Charles, Donald, George, and Ray were out doing who knew what to figure out what happened to Dee, and the boys had finally worn themselves out and were fast asleep. Miss Irene stretched herself out on the sofa and had already began to "Call hogs" —a term used to indicate when someone was in a deep sleep and snored so loud it sounded like the howl of a pig—while a restless Molly and Pearl sat at the kitchen table over coffee they didn't need.

"No, it's alright. I want to."

Pearl let it go. Maybe it was best to just let her talk.

"Susie LockLear was a slave, but that ain't all she was."

Molly laughed, but joy did not release itself into the room like it usually did when someone laughed. Instead, it held back as Molly unloaded Pandora's box. She continued.

"My grandmamma wasn't well. I guess slavery, it did something to her head. They say she saw things, went places, and spoke to people who weren't there—"

"Oh Molly, you really don't have to. You ain't got to prove nothing to me. I ain't ya judge now," said Pearl, but Molly kept going.

"Susie experienced hallucinations and delusions, but no one knew what it was. She...she even aborted her own grandbaby."

"I'm sorry," Pearl took Molly's hand in hers.

"She did it because she said she didn't want Massa Salal to take the baby. Even though slavery was over by the time Maxine was born, my mother, Susie was convinced that he would come and take away her children. No one knew what was wrong with her and when she was pregnant with Mom, the family feared it. Would Maxine grow up to be like her mother?"

Molly paused, "To an extent she did. But I—I was different and Grandmother hated me for it."

"How did you find out? About your grandmother?"

"Grandmamma had a brother, my great Uncle Bob. They weren't very close, only saw him a few times, but he liked to tell stories."

"I see."

"At the time, they didn't really have a name for it. All's they could say was that it was a brain disorder."

"Before she died, years after I'd run off with Dee," Molly's voice cracked at the mention of his name, and Pearl rubbed her back.

"It's alright."

"She was admitted to Ellisville. Not the new facility, but the old plantation it replaced. I never told nobody this, but that there's where she died."

Pearl didn't have to ask; everyone knew what Ellisville was. The Mississippi State Insane Asylum was the talk of many when it opened January 8, 1855. It was the first state institution for the mentally ill in Mississippi. After the First World War, two separate events affected the institution. First, a separate institution for the feeble-minded opened in 1921. Feeble-Minded, like poverty stricken, was a code word for Negroes deemed unfit for society. At the height of The Eugenics Movement, The Mississippi School and Colony for the Feeble-Minded removed children and adults deemed feeble-minded from their homes and from society.

"Susie suffered from Ictal Headaches, headaches associated with seizure activity in the brain or at least that's what they told us. They believed it developed from trauma."

Pearl could do nothing but shake her head. She knew Molly had to get this off her chest and decided to do less talking than usual.

"They were never able to connect the headaches to schizophrenia, since schizophrenia does not cause seizures, or at least they haven't found a direct correlation. But what they did find was that epilepsy, seizures that are often misdiagnosed as migraines (which Susie had) can sometimes produce symptoms that are similar to schizophrenia."

"Why now?"

"Pearl, we have to find Nora. Who knows if the migraines she experiences is the early stages of Ictal? I don't know what I'd do if something happened to her and I wasn't there to save her."

There was silence as the rain tapped against the windowsill, and the women were quiet a long time.

"I think that's why Grandma acted the way that she did. To really think about it, she wasn't that mean of a woman, just fearful.

"So, she tried to keep you away from the world," said Pearl.

"Exactly. She never wanted me to go anywhere. Like she was afraid something would happen to me. Held in bondage by fear, she was never able to appreciate that I was not like my mother. Instead, she sheltered me. Pearl—"

Molly stopped and looked at her friend, holding her gaze.

— "I was her slave."

CHAPTER THIRTY

FRANK

AUGUST 19, 1922
EARLIER THAT DAY

"EY, MAN, WHERE YOU GOING?" DON'T CHICKEN OUT ON ME NOW," said Oscar, his legs cocked as he stared down at the checker board. The wind rattled the sign-post to the General Store, and the porch screamed from Frank's heavy boots as he jumped off the porch and down the road.

"I catch you next time, man!" he yelled over his shoulder.

"Now ain't this a—" murmured Oscar.

The wind was strong against Frank's back as the clouds gathered together, darkening the sky on an otherwise sunny day.

Frank had a sixth sense about the weather. He believed there was more to it than snow and rain. He never understood why people complained when water fell from the sky, purifying the air and nourishing the soil. Indeed, the voice of the Almighty was in the thunder and he spoke clear through the rain. At least that's how Frank saw things. So, when Dee brought home the pretty Indian-looking girl some years back and the wind rattled the sign-post of the general store the moment she gave birth, he knew then that things would be different for The White's. He knew then that from her would come *the one*.

The Sheriffs waved from their rolled down window, wearing a smirk as the vehicle zoomed down the road. Frank picked up speed, running down Spring Ridge Road and headed to Clara's Place.

Seeing Gideon come out of the house cuffed, Frank stopped and hid behind the house on the corner, watching as Molly fell onto the ground, and two women held her back. He recognized Miss Irene, but didn't know who the big-boned woman was. He scanned the area, watching as people stood outside their homes to see what was going on. A little boy came onto the porch of the house and Frank ducked down, but it was too late.

"Hey!" said the boy. Frank sized him up to be seven or eight.

"Shh. Quiet."

"What you doing by my house?" said the boy.

"I said quiet. Come here."

"Why?"

"Boy, if you don't come here."

The boy huffed and puffed, knowing he'd better listen before the man told his mom. He jumped down the steps and came over to the side of the house.

"You see that woman over there?" Frank pointed to Molly in the distance. Next to her was Walter and Eddy.

"Yea, so?"

"Tell your mama they daddy said he wants her to go over there and take those two boys into the house."

"Why, you they daddy?"

"Boy, gone before I get my switch."

"OK, OK," said the boy, running back around the house, "Ma, hey, Ma!"

Frank looked at the sky; it was getting darker. The rain would fall soon. He waited. Now wasn't a good time.

Shortly, he saw a young woman approach Walter and Eddy, ushering them on into the house. Smiling, Frank looked on as the Sheriffs drove off with Dee in the backseat.

His attention was called back when he saw the big-boned woman run off. He decided to leave his hiding place and walking up closer, he saw that she was approaching Charles. This was as good a time as any.

The droplets of rain began to slip from the sky a few at a time as Frank walked over to the Whites, past the Oak Tree and closer to the house until he caught Charles' eye. Noticing the look of discontent in his eyes, he moved quickly, he'd only have a few seconds to do it.

"Nora is in danger," he said, walking past Charles and on back down the road, lifting the hood to his jacket over his head as the water fell from the sky.

CHAPTER THIRTY-ONE

"NORA!"

Lisa had a feeling Nora wasn't going to make it to the kitchen. She got on her knees and placed her ear over Nora's mouth. Still breathing.

"Nora? Nora, can you hear me?"

She looked around the room in a panic; she could have sworn she heard someone at the door, but it could have been her own heart pounding.

"Hold on Nora, I'm coming," she said, racing to the kitchen, snatching the towel from the table, and drenching it in water before running back to Nora lying on the living room floor passed out. Her body still; chest heaving in and out.

"Was she sleeping?" Lisa's mind raced, and sweat collected on the palms of her hands. The apartment rang with a silent loudness, the uninvited guest of sadness lingering in the spaces where sounds should have been. The constant murmur of her own thoughts replacing her friend's laughter and the whine of "what if" dripping from the towel now immersing the face of her friend. "Friend." The letters to the word spelled themselves out above her head, a manifestation of guilt.

Carl. She hated the man more than she loved the taste of hooch on her tongue, but now was not the time to be selfish. She needed him more so than she did Tanya, seeing no voodoo priestess in Harlem could help Nora anyway. She would know, having laced Nora's drink with the woman's very own herbs.

Descendant of the Igbo, Lisa laughed in the face of American medicine, a copied and less potent version of the African rites. She laughed, shaking her head at the girl's naiveté. Nora divulged every corner of her life, but never once asked Lisa about hers. Not about her origins in New Orleans before stealing her way on a New York train. Not about her abandonment of both mother and father. Not about how she had to pay rent on her back, the dripping sweat of old men she ignored long enough for the money to collect inside her body. No, she'd never divulged the details of her 30-year wretched experience.

Lisa stopped wiping at Nora's face and frowned, and anger crept into her pupils and turned them from dark brown to the darkest black. *Silly woman.* How stupid of her to run away from the plush life of acres of land and a family who loved her. That was Nora's problem all along, conceited. Lisa's hands trembled at the thought. Look at her, all laid out on the floor. That's what she got for thinking she was better than everyone else. Lisa stood and smiled. *It worked. I can't believe it worked!*

She scanned the table where the empty glass sat. It was only a matter of time before it became easy to get Nora hooked on her *special* tea. Watching Nora parade her good life in her face, her happiness and stupid pride. She'd resisted the inclination to do it sooner. But consistency was key if this was going to work. Lisa wiped away the tears of bitter jealousy that caught her between a rock and the American dream she sought to steal right from underneath Nora's nose. *Oh well.* It wasn't her fault, it was America's. As far as Lisa was concerned, Negroes were victims of White America. Had the constitution proved itself true, she reasoned, she would not find herself in this position. Besides, why should she be locked out of all that was good? It was because of her that Nora had made it this far after all.

Lisa approached the door and looked back at her friend, or was that the appropriate term after what she'd done? Her friend, a breathing zombie on the floor. The regret caught in Lisa's throat, holding her there with her hands on the doorknob. Tears rose from guilt stains inside her until the shame turned into hatred all over again. "Sorry, girl," she said, walking out of the room, carefully closing the door behind her. The train was arriving for Harlem in ten minutes; it was Friday and *The Savoy* was gonna be packed.

Thank you for reading part one of my book!

It would mean a great deal to me if you could give me your opinion. Not only will this let me know what you feel about my writing in general, but potential readers will also value your feedback.

If you have purchased this book from **Amazon,** *you will already have an account that will enable you to review books that you have purchased, or have been given as a gift. Just scroll down to Customer Reviews >* **Write a Customer Review***. If you have not purchased the book (received it as a gift) please mention this at the front end of the review so that it will be published.* **https://www.amazon.com**

Goodreads *is an excellent site for readers, and you can sign in with Facebook or sign up with an email address. This gives you access to thousands of books, enables you to connect with readers of the genres you enjoy, and leave reviews on any books that you have read and feel you would like to offer constructive comments.* **https://www.goodreads.com/***.* I would love for you to leave your review there as well.

Finally, I would be delighted to hear from you by email (**yecheilyah@yecheilyahysrayl.com**) *about the book.*

Your feedback is golden! Thank you.

ABOUT THE AUTHOR

Yecheilyah is the author of *The Stella Trilogy*, the novel *The Aftermath*, the play *Pearls Before Swine Vol. 1*, and three collections of poetry: *From the Depths of a Woman's Heart, From When I was a Black Girl*, and *From Girlhood to Womanhood*.

An Independent Author, Blogger, Poet and Book Reviewer, Yecheilyah is the founder of Literary Korner Publishing, the publishing company under which she publishes her books, LK Pub. Writer's Workshop, and The PBS Blog. She has been writing for eighteen years and publishing for ten years. She has reviewed over 20 books, written over 20 articles and facilitates Author Interviews for Independent Authors on her blog.

Yecheilyah writes Literary Fiction, Poetry and whatever else her mind conceives, full time. Originally from Chicago, IL, she lives with her husband and is currently working to publish *Revelation: The Nora White Story (Book Two)*.

www.yecheilyahysrayl.com

Made in the USA
San Bernardino, CA
25 July 2018